STEPS OF THE CALLEJON

Jane Zhang

First printing, November, 2016

ISBN: 978-0-9979255-0-0

Cover design by Tamara Garza
Typeface: Garamond

Printed in the United States of America.

In memory of Anival

Acknowledgements

I would like to gratefully acknowledge the people who have helped make this book a reality. First, I want to thank Birgit Shorack for planting the idea for this book in my head when she said that no one ever writes about the day-to-day of missionary life.

I owe a debt of gratitude to my editor Meghan Ward, who, with her sharp eye for detail and keen observations, helped turn my manuscript into *Steps of the Callejon*.

Tamara Garza, you are amazing! Thank you for creating a book cover that captures feel of the *barrios* so well. (We shouldn't judge a book by its cover, but we know we all do!)

To my husband Matt, thank you for your belief in me even though I didn't let you read the manuscript for four years.

I also want to thank all my friends and family who never failed to believe this book will happen, including those who supported the Kickstarter campaign to launch this book into the universe.

Finally, I am so deeply gratefully to my ministry team and my neighbors and friends in Venezuela. The time I spent with you transformed my life. Through you, God came into my world.

STEPS OF THE CALLEJON

Prologue

In many Latin American Countries, the word *barrio* means neighborhood. In Caracas, Venezuela, the word *barrio* refers to the slums on the hillsides surrounding the city. People in the city view these *barrios* as breeding grounds of crime. But for you, who are poor, a *barrio* is a foothold into the economic opportunities a large city provides and a safe haven in a sea of three million people. The *barrio* is home.

A new *barrio* will be made up of *ranchitos*, plywood shacks hammered together with a few nails and glued together with dreams. A *ranchito* will be one of many located alongside an existing road or footpath called a *callejon*. These *callejones* weave themselves up and down the hillsides and, more often than not, the *callejon* steps of a new *barrio* are made of dirt rather than concrete. If your *ranchito* is next to an existing road, then perhaps there is a light pole from which you can tap electricity. There is also a likelihood that water pipes run along the road, and you can tap into that as well.

Once you have lived in your *ranchito* for a while, you start losing your fears of being chased off by the police for illegally squatting on government land or of the ground sinking or sliding off the hillside after a heavy rainstorm. Then you start scraping together money to buy concrete for a floor or some cinder blocks to build a wall or two. You are not in a rush. The progression from laying the foundation to finishing the house never ends because you can always tack on a room or build another floor.

As you build your house, you also start building your family. Your relatives hear that you have a place in the city, so they send their sons and daughters your way. You are happy because you hope the extra pairs of hands will help with the household expenses. Even if they do not, you are still happy, because they are family. So you squeeze them into your house. They share a room with your children or sleep on the sofa.

The foundation of a *barrio* is faith. It is faith that draws you to the *barrio*. It is faith that gets you up each morning to look for work. It is faith that lies in bed next to you at night while you wait for your loved ones to return home safely. You have learned that "Faith is the assurance of things hoped for and the conviction of things not seen."

"¡Ojalá!" you say at the beginning of each sentence and of each hope and desire. *"Ojalá, God willing."*

Barrio Map

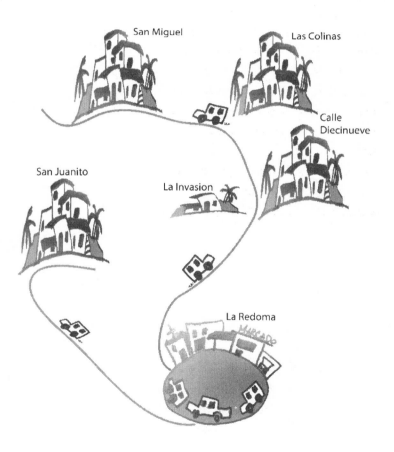

Part I

The Barrios

Jeeps rumbling
Weaving up steep broken asphalt

Girls dolled up
Flying down the hills on backseats of motorcycles
Heads tucked between shoulder blades of strapping young men

Roosters crowing
Dogs barking
Cats skittering across tin roofs chasing black birds

Sun-dried laundry dancing on top of rooftops
To the rhythm of reggaeton
Swaying along
With tangled limbs of lovers in dark dank rooms
With specks of dust dancing on thin golden poles of light
Beaming through crevices in cinder block walls

Is that Lucita pattering down the alley behind her abuela,
Her dress fluttering above her bare feet?
Is that Ramón leaning against his iron gate,
Silently watching the hours go by?

¡Lucita, mi amor!
Ramón, Buenos. ¡¿cómo estás?!

Come, join me in the barrio hills
Squeeze into the jeeps and ascend the slopes

Climb up the steps of the callejon
Enter the rooms filled
With life
With tears
With laughter

Days in the Barrios

JOYCE CHEN WAITS at the base of the hill outside the Redoma food market. She is waiting for Thomas Reed, the lanky leader of the small ragamuffin band of missionaries in Caracas she has been a part of for the past year. *Camionetas* fly past, leaving behind the grumbles of tired engines and exhaust. The sky darkens. The air feels heavy, signaling an impending afternoon storm. Passengers get off and on the *camionetas*, pausing briefly to glance at the ominous clouds and praying that the sky will not open until they make it safely to their homes.

A blue *camioneta* stops at the unmarked bus stop. No Thomas. Joyce continues to wait with one eye on the sky, praying that the rain will hold off until they make it up the hill for their weekly visit with the Aguilas, the only family in the *barrio* San Juanito that has welcomed their friendship and showed interest in exploring and deepening their understanding and faith in Jesus.

Finally, Thomas's lanky figure fills the doorway of a faded yellow *camioneta*. After greeting each other, Joyce follows Thomas up the steep steps into San Juanito. She tries to keep up with Thomas while avoiding the trash and dog waste littering the narrow *callejon*. Despite having followed Thomas countless times up these steps, Joyce still struggles to match his stride.

\#

Sara Sanchez de Aguila is distracted when Joyce and Thomas arrive at her door. She is talking with her neighbor, who is also her stepmother's brother-in-law, about the health of her half-sister's daughter who lives a couple of houses down. Sara greets Joyce and Thomas with the customary kisses on the right cheek and waves them inside without pausing in conversation with her neighbor.

Joyce sits down on the couch facing the whirring of a small, uncovered three-blade fan to cool off. Thomas sits down on the wooden stool beside the couch. They patiently wait for Sara.

Minutes later, Sara greets Thomas and Joyce again in the living room: kisses on the right cheek.

"Adan is not home. He is at a job he got earlier today to fix the washing machine of a lady who lives in the *barrio* above yours," Sara says.

Before Thomas or Joyce has a chance to invite Sara to sit down, she excuses herself to the kitchen to make her guests *cafecitos*. Joyce and Thomas wait.

Sara is running low on coffee. Prices have skyrocketed ever since the coffee farmers went on strike right after the government proposed to cap the price on coffee. Sara pours boiling water over the last of the ground coffee in a handheld cloth filter. Then she adds enough powdered milk and sugar to compensate for the weakness of the coffee. She sighs. The powdered milk and sugar are also running low. She hopes Adan will make enough today for these extra items she will need to buy on market day.

When the *cafecitos* are ready, Sara brings them down with a large crusty chunk of white *campesino* bread covering the mouth of each mismatched cup. She hands her guests their coffee with a gracious smile. She watches as her guests dip the bread in the sugary coffee, enjoying the sweet treat.

Once Sara settles herself down on the couch among her guests, Thomas speaks.

"How are you doing?" he asks Sara.

"Not so well. I don't know what to do with the situation at work. My *jefe* hasn't paid me for three weeks now. Should I ask her again? I don't want to irritate her. She'll pay, won't she?" Her eyes cloud with concern as she continues. "Daniel is sick. He was coughing all night. I took him to the clinic down in the Redoma, but the doctor said, 'It's just a cold' and gave me the same medicine that did not work before. I'm trying the stuff Joyce's neighbor, Evanglin, gave me when all the families from the different *barrios* met up at the *convivencia* last week. She said her youngest son, Raúl, had the same kind of cough and fever, and the stuff worked for him.

"My brother-in-law just lost his job. He's home all the time now, drinking. He is driving my sister, Edna, crazy." Sara's eyes narrow with anger as she describes her sister's situation. "They don't have any more money. My sister has started selling *chucherias* out of her house, but how much can you make selling chips and *chicles* when you live so high up the *callejon*? She doesn't have enough neighbors up there. She often brings her daughters over around dinnertime, but those girls need to eat good meals three times a day."

Sara sighs and adds, "And I just found out from my uncle that my niece's cancer has spread. She is now waiting to see if the government can fly her to Cuba for treatment. *¡Ojalá!* She'll be able to go soon.

"I also had trouble sleeping last night because of the ruckus outside. Did you hear about the shooting last night? It happened just a few steps up the *callejon*."

Thomas and Joyce listen to Sara tell the stories of life in San Juanito. They take each story and hold it in their hearts, sharing in Sara's burden. They feel the powerlessness of a manual laborer who is at the mercy of her boss, the despair of a mother worried for her child's health, the frustration of a wife whose husband cannot provide, and the fear of a family held captive in cycles of poverty and violence.

Outside, a gentle sprinkle has turned into a downpour. Streams of water carry debris from the top of the hill, clogging gutters at the bottom, cleansing the *callejon* of filth.

Sara turns on the light. The single lightbulb dangles by a thin wire in the middle of the ceiling, illuminating the faces of family and visitors sitting together around the living room as if it's a warm fire.

Hours pass. The rain outside has stopped. It is time for Thomas and Joyce to leave. The visitors stand up and bid farewell to Sara.

"Till next week."

"Till next week."

Kisses on the cheeks.

They step out of Sara's house and carefully walk down the *callejon*'s uneven steps, slick with engine grease and rain. Joyce is silent. As a Christian missionary, she ponders the mystery of God's plan for Sara's life in the midst of so much suffering. *What is the will of God in the lives of those we visit?* she wonders. She is perplexed about God's plan for her as as well. *What is the will of God for my days in the barrios as I witness such suffering? Does my presence bring Sara any comfort?*

\#

Joyce makes her way back to her *barrio*, Calle Diecinueve, back to her little apartment she shares with Amelia Jones, her housemate, teammate, friend is sitting at the table.

"*Hola.* How are Sara and the kids?" Amelia asks.

"Same things: illness, poverty and crime," Joyce sighs.

Amelia gives an empathetic nod and lifts some of the burden Joyce has carried home from San Juanito.

\#

After Joyce puts down her things, she goes to the kitchen to make dinner. She boils a pot of water for pasta and chops up garlic, onions, tomatoes and zucchinis for a vegetable spaghetti sauce.

A knock at the door startles the roommates. They are not expecting anyone.

"*¿Quién es?*" Amelia calls out.

"¡Evangelin!" their neighbor from upstairs responds.

"*¡Ya va!*" Amelia says as she gets up to open the door. "I'm coming."

"*¡Hola!*" Amelia greets. "*¿Cómo estás?*"

"*¡Bien, Bien! ¡Hola, Amelia! Hola, Yoli!*" Evangelin replies when she sees Amelia and Joyce at the door.

Evangelin Gomez de Suza steps down into the apartment her husband, Enrique, built a few years back to rent out to supplement their income. Her sons, Raúl and Ángel, tumble down the steps after their mother, finding their seats in the laps of Evangelin and Amelia as they sit down at the table. Joyce finds a few sheets of paper and markers to occupy the boys. Five-year-old Raúl grins at no one in particular and gets to work coloring a masterpiece of his imagination. His older brother Ángel, intent on participating in the adult conversation, leaves the markers untouched.

"Would you like a *cafecito*?" Amelia offers.

"*Sí, gracias,*" Evangelin says.

Joyce, already standing at the stove, puts a small pot on the stove to heat up water for the coffee and listens to the conversation between Evangelin and Amelia.

Evangelin has had a long day. After work, she had to go to class in Los Telares.

"An hour away?"

"An hour away."

"How many buses did you have to take?"

"Three. I can't wait until they finish the subway extension to Los Telares. The traffic between here and there in the afternoons is impossible!"

"Do you know when the extension will be completed?"

"The papers say in half a year, but of course there will be delays."

Evangelin arrived home late in the evening. She still has not cooked dinner for her family, but she wanted to stop by to say "hi." For Evangelin, company is more nourishing than food.

"We haven't eaten dinner yet either. Would you like to stay?"

"No, no. Thank you, though."

"Are you sure? It wouldn't be any trouble. You're always feeding us. Let us feed you today."

"Yes, we just started cooking. It wouldn't be any trouble," Joyce echoes Amelia's invitation from the kitchen.

Ángel looks eagerly at his mom, hoping for the opportunity to hang out with his *gringa* and *chinita* neighbors a bit longer.

"Well, ok. Only if you have enough," Evangelin finally relents. Ángel flashes everyone a big toothy smile.

"*¡Por supuesto!*" Amelia and Joyce say together. Glad she can serve in a concrete way, Joyce takes out a couple more tomatoes and zucchinis from the refrigerator and portions out more dry pasta to boil.

Bombas

JOYCE BOLTS AWAKE. It is 6 am. The *bomba* truck is scheduled to exchange gas tanks today. She quickly pulls on a pair of jeans, throws on a T-shirt, and slips her feet into the black Old Navy flip flops she picked up during her last trip in the States.

She pulls the empty *bomba* out from under the sink, detaches the gas line from the stove, unlocks the door and climbs up the stairs to the top of her *callejon*. A few other neighbors are already waiting. Jeeps rush by, carrying the first of the commuters down the hill.

"Has the truck come by yet?" Joyce asks no one in particular.

Standing a few steps away and still in her nightgown, Yasmin answers, "It went up the hill about a half hour ago. It should be back anytime now."

Joyce is glad to see Yasmin this morning. She and Yasmin have developed a unique rapport over the past year. Both slightly overweight, they joke and tease one another mercilessly.

"I've never met a fat *chinita*," Yasmin joked once.

"And I have yet to see a skinny Venezuelan," Joyce retorted.

"How long have you been waiting?" Joyce asks Yasmin.

"About 45 minutes."

"How's school?"

"It's going all right."

As much as Joyce wants to develop her friendship with Yasmin, she has resigned herself to what Yasmin is willing to offer. Amelia has been more successful in befriending Yasmin. Joyce will take the bantering and leave the befriending to Amelia.

The iron door at the corner *abasto* across the street cracks open, and Alfredo, the grocer, with eyes bloodshot, appears behind the doors. He waves to the growing crowd waiting for the *bomba* truck.

"Morning, Alfredo."

"Is there chicken today?"

"Are you baking *guavaba* bread this afternoon?"

"Had a good time last night?" one of the guys waiting for the *bomba* truck teases, hinting at the one-too-many Polar beers Alfredo and his pals drank the previous night.

From up the hill, the "cling, cling, cling" of the *bomba* truck is finally heard as it descends. The guys standing in the bed of the truck bang on the empty *bombas*, needlessly calling the attention of those who have been waiting for them since early morning. When the truck finally stops at the top of the *callejon*, one of the guys jumps down and starts tossing the empty *bombas* lined up at the feet of the neighbors to a guy standing in the truck bed, poised to catch them. Another worker standing in the bed of the truck hands down full *bombas* to the last member of the crew. Joyce crowds closer to the truck and waits her turn, grateful she has not missed it. The spare *bomba* under her kitchen sink only has enough gas for a couple more days, not enough to last till the next delivery.

When all the *bombas* have been exchanged, the neighbors disperse back down the *callejon* and disappear into their homes.

The Baker

ALFREDO ESCOBAR OPENS his oven and rotates the trays of *campesino* bread. He returns his attention to the dough rising on the counter. The neighbors will be waking up from noon naps soon and will be lining up in front of his *abasto*.

"So you built the ovens yourself?" Joyce asks.

"*Sí, por supuesto*. Ovens cost too much. Even the used ones cost ten times as much as what I've spent building these two. Plus, I don't have that much space here. It was easier and cheaper to rig my own than spend a fortune on equipment that doesn't fit. I have to watch the bread more closely because the heat doesn't distribute as evenly, but I've got it down to a rhythm." Alfredo says as he reaches for Joyce's hands and does a quick salsa step.

Alfredo never stops dancing. During the day, he dances with his bread; in the evenings, he dances with his neighbors and kids; at night, he dances with his wife while the rest of the house sleeps.

"When did you start baking bread?"

"I learned my skills at the Caracas Hilton and started baking here a few years back. At first, I baked just for my family. Then everyone in the neighborhood wanted to buy bread from me, especially around Christmas. I make the best *guavaba* bread and *pan de jamon*. The secret is using twice as much butter and hand kneading the dough. Or perhaps, they just wanted to save themselves a trip down the hill." Alfredo shrugs and smiles.

Alfredo portions out the dough and starts stretching and rolling out the next batch of *campesinos* for the oven.

"So what's a *chinita* doing in these *barrios*?" He asks Joyce.

"I'm here with Tomas and Agnes. We are a group of *misionerios.*" Joyce answers.

"And what do you guys do?"

"We prayerfully seek ways to share the love of Christ by caring for our neighbors in the marginal communities of society."

"And how do you do that?"

"By coming alongside them in prayer and supporting and advocating for their dreams." Joyce answers tentatively.

"And how do you do that?" Alfredo pries the *chinita* a bit more.

"Honestly, I'm still praying about what that looks like. I came down to Venezuela with a master's degree in international economic development. I thought I could do a quick assessment of the economic opportunities available in the *barrios* and help people start and maintain successful businesses."

"And how is that going?"

"A lot slower and more complicated than I thought. Most people I've talked to have dreams of starting something, but no one seems to move in that direction. There are always more pressing issues. I've been to a couple of the government microfinance loan meetings, and it sounds like the majority of the borrowers default on their loans because they use the money on home improvements and family emergencies more than on their businesses. Then the government comes and repossesses their furniture and whatnot because that is the only collateral they had. I'm not sure if these micro-loans are helping anyone out."

"I took out a couple of those before."

"How did it go?"

"Good, I used them to build my ovens."

"Are you going to apply for more?"

"They want me to. I guess I'm their poster child. I want to start a *panaderia* one day."

"Your bread is way tastier and cheaper than the bread they sell at the Redoma. You'd be so successful if you opened up down there!" Joyce says enthusiastically.

"Perhaps one day." Julio says.

"What do you need to move in that direction?" Joyce probes.

"*No sé.* I haven't thought too much about it. Right now, I'm enjoying baking bread for my neighbors."

"How much do you sell a week? Are you thinking about raising your prices any time soon? It is way cheaper than how much it costs down at the *panaderia.*"

"*No sé.* For now, I enjoy baking and selling my bread to my neighbors at a price they can pay." Alfredo answers.

"*Bueno*, I know I really appreciate your bread." Joyce says trying to keep the disappoint out of her voice.

Alfredo turns to the ovens and pulls out tray after tray of golden crusted *campesinos*. He carefully picks one up and pulls it apart, handing a steaming hot chunk to Joyce.

"*¡Bien provecho, la chinita!* May God bless you in your mission."

"*Ójala.*" Joyce toasts Alfredo with the bread.

Guests, Part I

DULIMAR RUNS DOWN the *callejon* steps of San Juanito with her baby sister in her arms. She peers into Sara's window through the iron bars.

"Sara! Sara!" She waits for someone to reply.

"¡Ya va! ¿Quién es?" Sara shouts back.

"It's Dulimar."

Sara shuffles to the window and looks out, *"¿Qué quieres?"* she asks.

"Mi mamá," Dulimar whispers through her tears. "She's sick. She hasn't moved or spoken all day."

"¿Qué? What happened?" Sara asks.

"She had been complaining of a headache for the past week. Then this morning, she slipped and fell when she went out on her way to the outhouse. We got her to bed, but she hasn't gotten up or made a sound since. She just stares at the wall even when my brother and I call to her and shake her," Dulimar's voice trembles.

"Ya va," Sara says as she leaves the window and reappears a few seconds later at the door.

"Come in. Have you had anything to eat?" Sara asks Dulimar as she ushers the girl inside.

"No. None of us has eaten since last night," Dulimar replies, suddenly aware of the growling emptiness inside her.

"Well, have a seat while I get you something to eat," Sara says, mothering over Dulimar. She places a hand gently on her shoulder and guides the child to the living room.

When Dulimar's eyes adjust to the darkness of the room, she finds herself before a *gringo* audience. She instinctively holds her baby sister closer and looks at the *gringos* in timid surprise. She recognizes them and has gone to their kids club, where she played games and listened to stories, but she has never been this close or vulnerable to them before. *"Hola."* Thomas and Joyce greet Dulimar. *"Cómo estás?"*

"Bien," Dulimar replies in a whisper.

Sara introduces the girl. "This is Dulimar. She's the daughter of Yolanda, who lives at the top of the *callejon.*"

Sara wants to share more about Yolanda with her guests. She knows they would be interested in Yolanda's story, but she will hold her tongue until Dulimar leaves.

"I am sorry to hear that your mom is sick," Joyce says, wanting to help Dulimar carry some of her worries.

"Has she seen a doctor yet?" Thomas asks.

"No, my mom stayed home all week."

"Has anyone gone for a doctor?" Sara asks, concerned that Yolanda is not getting the medical help she needs.

"My aunt called and said she will come by tomorrow morning and take her to the hospital," Dulimar says.

"That's probably best," Sara says. "Our *Cubano* left a couple of months ago, and the government hasn't sent us a replacement yet. If we need anything, we have to go to the clinic in the Redoma, and the line there is always wrapped around the building. It sounds like Yolanda's sister has made arrangements for Yolanda to go straight to the hospital and get looked at."

"Your mom's going to be fine," Sara tells Dulimar. "She'll see the doctor tomorrow and get help at the hospital."

Sara gets up and goes to the kitchen. After a few minutes, she reappears with a ham and cheese sandwich and a cup of milky coffee for the girl.

"Gracias," Dulimar says and eagerly reaches out for the food and drink. Before feeding herself, she breaks off small pieces of the sandwich and feeds them to the baby in her arms.

When she finishes, she hands the plate and cup back to Sara and says goodbye, timidly receiving the farewell kisses the *gringos* offer.

Dulimar lifts her baby sister back on her hip and slowly climbs up the *callejon* a bit lighter, knowing the burden she bore alone is now shared among many.

#

After Dulimar leaves, Sara turns to her guests, eager to share Yolanda's story.

"Yolanda lives at the top of the *callejon*," Sara begins. "She has lived there for many years and has been a difficult woman for her neighbors to get along with. The three kids she has are from three different men." Sara pauses and lets this information sink in before adding the juiciest bit of detail for her guests.

"She is a *bruja*!"

Curious to know more about Yolanda's background, Thomas and Joyce ask Sara questions she is eager to answer.

"What kind of work does Yolanda do?"

"Why don't her neighbors like her?"

"How long has she dabbled in witchcraft?"

After Sara has painted a more complete picture of Yolanda in their minds, Thomas suggests they go up to Yolanda's after they are done with their visit at Sara's.

#

Thomas and Joyce follow Sara up the *callejon* steps, stopping every so often as Sara greets the neighbors leaning out of their windowsills and against their doorways to update them on Yolanda. The neighbors, as curious as Thomas and Joyce, seek out more details and offer their opinions and condolences.

"What happened?"

"She hasn't gotten out of bed since morning?"

"Her place is a mess, no wonder."

"All that rain last night."

"Poor kids."

"Too bad the *Cubano* left. It'll be hard for her to get checked out."

"Can't she go to the hospital?"

"Who's going to take her?"

"She probably just needs to rest."

"It's that witchcraft she dabbles in."

"She has finally gone completely crazy."

When the three finally make it up to the top of the hill, Sara knocks on the front gate and yells out, "Dulimar!"

They do not have to wait long. Dulimar, with a look of relief on her face, cracks open the gate to let the visitors in. The visitors make their way past the outhouse and follow Dulimar up the slippery uneven steps to the rickety plywood *ranchito*.

The house is dark and smells of mildew mixed with the heavy weight of incense. Piles of clothes cover broken dressers and chairs.

Dulimar goes directly to Yolanda.

"*¡Mamá!*" Dulimar shouts into Yolanda's ear. "We have guests!"

Yolanda stars vacantly into space, responding neither to her daughter's voice nor her tugs and pulls. A boy, about four years old, joins Dulimar in calling and shaking Yolanda. "*¡Mamá! ¡Mamá!*" Both children's voices become more and more desperate. Their eyes, wet with tears, plead with their mother to respond.

The baby, lying next to Yolanda, senses the tension and anxiety in the air and cries out in fear.

Joyce walks over to the bed and picks up the baby. She cradles her in her arms and gently sings and rocks the baby from side to side while Sara pulls the children off of their mother.

"*Ya. Ya.* It'll be okay," Sara coos. "It'll be okay."

The night slips in. A candle is lit, casting long flickering shadows on the thin smoke-stained walls, creating an eerie atmosphere in the cramped little room.

"Perhaps we should pray," Thomas suggests.

"Yes, that's a good idea," Sara says.

Thomas wants Sara to understand what he is about to pray, so he takes a minute to explain. "Sometimes, these kinds of things have a spiritual element. From what you said about the witchcraft, it is not unlikely that this might have a demonic component in it. I'm going to pray for a casting out of evil spirits. Something might happen, or it might not. We'll see. If anything happens, do not be afraid."

Sara nods. She is familiar with the spiritual battles fought in the households of her *barrio*. She draws Dulimar and the little boy closer to her.

Joyce, trusting in the guidance of her team leader, watches and hopes to witness a miracle like the ones she has only read or heard about secondhand. Her heart beats with the anticipation of witnessing a demon casted out. Thomas begins to pray. "God, we thank you that you are here with us. We pray for Yolanda, that you might heal her, physically as well as spiritually. We pray for your protection of these children. You know Yolanda, all her thoughts, all her actions. We pray for your compassion and grace. Come and heal her."

Thomas turns to Yolanda and calls out to her. "Yolanda! Yolanda!"

He waits for her to respond. Yolanda moans.

"Yolanda! Yolanda!" Thomas calls again.

The children join in, "*¡Mamá! ¡Mamá!*"

Yolanda moans again and turned toward the wall, away from the cacophony of voices.

After a few minutes of not receiving a response, Thomas lays his hand on Yolanda's shoulder and finishes his prayer. "God, we pray for your healing. We pray that you reach Yolanda in her pain and darkness. We pray that your holy spirit will dwell in her, pushing out any presence of tormenting spirits. We thank you for your love and grace. In the name of Jesus we pray, Amen."

Amens echo around the room.

Joyce hugs the baby tight. She is disappointed the prayer did not awaken Yolanda. She also feels slightly let down that she did not witness a miraculous healing that she can tell others about.

"We will keep on praying for her," Thomas says to the others.

"*Sí*," Sara agrees, determined to be of help.

The visitors stay for a bit longer. They watch the candle burn slowly down before leaving.

"Come by tomorrow and let me know how your mom's doing," Sara instructs Dulimar.

"Ok," Dulimar replies, reluctantly letting go of Sara's arm.

Joyce whispers a prayer over the baby and hands her back to Dulimar. "*Chao, mi amor*," Joyce says to the child carrying burdens far too heavy for her small frame.

The visitors make their way out of the darkened *ranchito* and down the slippery steps to the front gate, wondering how anyone could make it down to the bottom of those steps without slipping.

Guests, Part II

YOLANDA LIMPS SLOWLY down the *callejon* steps. Night has fallen, and the *barrio* is quiet. She does not like to stay at home. It is too empty without her kids now that they are living with her sister.

She stops at a closed window and calls in.

"Sara!" she cries, hoping Sara will open the door to her and allow her to spend the night on her couch.

Hearing no sound inside, she continues down the steps. She finds herself in front of Sra. Francisca's house at the bottom of the hill. "Frani!" she calls.

Sra. Francisca opens the door and invites her in. "Yolanda, what are you doing out so late? Don't you know you are scaring everyone with your night wanderings? And where are your clothes? You can't walk around half-naked."

Standing in her threadbare nightgown, Yolanda makes no reply. She simply looks into Sra. Francisca's eyes and waits.

"Come in, come in." Sra. Francisca answers wearily. It has been a long day. She has had to make countless trips up and down the steep *callejon* steps, carrying supplies on her back like a mule for anyone paying her a few *bolívares*.

For years, she had to stay close to home to take care of her crippled sister. At the end of each day, she always managed to make enough money to feed her sister and herself. But since her sister passed away a couple months earlier, the loads she carries on her back have grown heavier and the *callejon* steps steeper.

Sra. Francisca ushers Yolanda into her apartment. She guides Yolanda to a chair and asks her if she wants something to eat. Hearing no response but seeing the hunger in Yolanda's eyes, Sra. Francisca goes over to the stove and heats a leftover *arepa* in the pan and hands it on a plate to Yolanda.

Yolanda takes the plate in her left hand while her right hand lies limply on her lap. She brings the plate up to her mouth, trying to maneuver the corn cake into her mouth with only her tongue and lips, but she fails. She cannot control her facial muscles. The twitches become more severe the harder she tries. Tears well in her eyes before falling down her face.

When Sra. Francisca sees Yolanda struggling, she pulls up a chair in front of Yolanda, takes the plate, breaks the *arepa* into pieces and feeds Yolanda one bite at a time. She watches patiently as Yolanda works the slack muscles in her jaws, trying to chew.

When Yolanda finally finishes the *arepa*, Sra. Francisca wipes the crumbs from the corners of Yolanda's mouth with her apron. Yolanda looks blankly at Sra. Francisca, like an innocent child waiting for instruction. Her face is absent of the bitterness that once etched the furrows of her brow and the contempt that darkened her eyes before she fell ill.

Looking into Yolanda's eyes, Sra. Francisca realizes that Yolanda is not capable of taking care of herself. Though the medicine the doctor gave to Yolanda has brought her out of bed, she has not fully recovered. Yolanda needs to go back to the community hospital for another full medical checkup, but she has no one to take her. She has heard that Yolanda's sister is coming to help take care of her, but that is not until the end of the week. Until then, someone has to look after her.

Yolanda's condition has quieted her loud diatribes against her children, against her neighbors, against God. Sra. Francisca reaches out and grabs Yolanda's hand. She leads her to the bedroom her sister had occupied.

Yolanda pulls off her nightgown and lies naked in the empty bed, falling fast asleep. Sra. Francisca brings down a blanket from the top of the dresser and covers the sleeping woman who has already begun to fill the void left by her sister.

Relationships

You surround me, entwine me in the veins of history
Warm me with embraces of laughter
And wash me with tears
I twirl in your arms in an unending dance
Elated, exhausted, unable to stop
We whirl across the years
Binding ourselves to each other
Tighter and tighter
In new and old patterns of fancy

Housemates

AFTER A LONG MORNING of errands, Amelia and Joyce enjoy uninterrupted peace on Evangelin's balcony above their apartment. Evangelin's family is out for the day visiting relatives. The girls have the place to themselves. They do not have to worry about Ángel and Raúl popping their heads out of their window, asking them to play.

They look over their valley, stacked with cinder block houses and plywood *ranchitos*. The girls have, between them on a makeshift table, a bottle of Casillero del Diablo and a plate of cheese. They are celebrating a successful day at Marco, the megastore with all the imported goodies too large to haul into the country in their suitcases. They have succeeded in getting a one-day membership so they can buy furniture for the office.

They also found a willing truck driver to transport their purchases to the office. This, they consider a greater miracle. The last time they ventured to Marco, they could not even find a taxi driver who would take them to their *barrio*. They were told repeatedly that their *barrio* was "*caliente*," hot with crime. The "heat wave" has apparently passed.

It is two in the afternoon. The *barrio* is quiet in its post-lunch stupor. Amelia refills the empty wine glasses and takes another sliver of cheese.

"¡Salud!"

"¡Salud!"

The girls clink their cups and slowly sip wine and nibble on cheese. The comfortable silence between them rests at their feet like a lazy orange tabby basking under the sun.

Minutes waltz by.

Amelia stretches out her legs in front of her and leans back against the wall. She looks over at Joyce, her partner in crime.

For Amelia, loneliness always prowls in the dark corners of every room. With Joyce there, the darkness is at least manageable. Joyce's presence in a room of Venezuelans assures her that she is not alone on this crazy journey into the unknown where she tries to bring love and grace into the lives of those who cross her path.

"What are you up to this afternoon?" Amelia asks.

"I'm thinking about heading up the *callejon* to Sra. Rosalia's. I promised I'd visit this week," Joyce answers, reluctantly shifting her thoughts to the obligations of the afternoon.

"You want to come?" Joyce probes, "They have been asking after you."

Bringing Amelia would mean brownie points for Joyce in the eyes of her host family. She envies and covets Amelia's social graces, her ability to draw curiosity and laughter out of all those around her.

In Amelia, Joyce sees the sophistication and tact she herself lacks but craves. As much as she would like to believe that she brings as much to the team as Amelia does, she cannot let go of the constant weight of inferiority that drags at her feet each time she walks into a room with Amelia. She believes Amelia is the quintessential missionary: whole and beautiful with blond highlights, blessed under the sublime light of celestial love. She, on the other hand, is Robin to Batman, Dr. Watson to Sherlock Holmes, with so many character flaws that her only witness is displaying her brokenness like battle scars fought and earned in the trenches between sin and grace.

Ever since Joyce arrived in Venezuela, she has tried to build meaningful relationships with each member of her host family. But as nice and welcoming as they are to her, she still feels from them the kind of politeness one shows to strangers, the only giving and never receiving kind of hospitality. She remains a guest despite having lived with them for three months. Perhaps, she has nothing to give.

She wishes her host family could accept her as one of their own the way Amelia's host family has accepted Amelia. They celebrate their joys and share their worries with Amelia and even demand her attendance at family functions.

For Joyce, the only exception is Sra. Rosalia, the matriarch of her host family. The petite white-haired lady always has a genuine smile to greet Joyce. Sra. Rosalia does not seem to mind her limited vocabulary or her lack of conversation skills. The *abuela* seems content simply with Joyce's presence to keep her company while her own kids and grandkids are out working or attending school.

"I can't. I have some work to finish up at the office," Amelia pulls Joyce's attention back to their conversation and excuses herself. She does not feel like being "on" this afternoon. Visits always tire Amelia. She believes it is her responsibility to present herself with a certain level of grace and kindness, to proactively engage with each person. Before each visit, she has learned to give herself time to mentally and emotionally prepare, to empty herself of her own concerns in order to fully hear and respond to the concerns of those she is visiting.

Amelia envies Joyce's courage to just be herself during visits. She has seen Joyce's unconscious vulnerability create a safe environment where others feel free to be vulnerable as well. This connectedness that Joyce achieves almost instantaneously with people, Amelia has to consciously cultivate.

"Ok, next time perhaps," Joyce says, not without a trace a disappointment. She will have to do the visit alone and face her fears of inadequacy.

"How is Sra. Rosalia doing?" Amelia asks, wanting to move past the awkwardness of saying "no."

"She's doing better," Joyce answers. "She was complaining of high blood pressure last week. Her kids constantly tell her to slow down, not to do so much. But that's who she is. She loves taking care of the house and the pets, fussing over her grandkids. As much as she complains, I think she thrives on it. I don't know what would happen if she actually took things more slowly."

The girls balance themselves on a fine wire of friendship and companionship, gingerly holding on to the complexity that binds them together. They help each other forward through the daily challenges they face, together and on their own.

The glasses are empty with no wine left in the bottle to refill them. With content sighs, the girls pick up their dishes and move toward what the day still has in store for them.

Host Family

LAUNDRY SWAYS GENTLY on the wires strung precariously outside of barred windows and on rooftops, drying under the blazing afternoon sun. It is that lazy time in the day when even the jeeps stop shuttling passengers up and down the steep hillsides. The scrawny *callejon* dogs are taking a break from scavenging and have returned to their napping spots in the shadows of the abandoned tireless trucks lining the stretch of no man's land between the *barrios*.

The afternoon sun drapes itself lazily across the rescued street mutt that is dreaming contentedly on Sra. Rosalia's toasty patio floor. In the corner of the room, the chatter of two parakeets occasionally disrupts the afternoon calm. Joyce sits in one of the two plastic woven lawn chairs on the patio and watches the hot iron in Sra. Rosalia's hands travel to and fro over the school uniforms of her grandsons. A pile of freshly dried clothes at the end of the ironing board waits patiently for its turn.

Joyce sips the last bit of the milky *cafecito* has Sra. Rosalia made for her. Having attempted but failed to find words to carry a conversation past the initial greeting, she allows herself to slip into an uninhibited restfulness under the warm presence of her Venezuelan grandmother.

"*Mi chinita*," Sra. Rosalia calls tenderly over her shoulders, about to ask a question before realizing Joyce has fallen asleep. She smiles and muses to herself. *This chinita appears in my world out of nowhere to keep me company on lazy afternoons. How peculiar she is to want to move here rather than stay with her own family. She is just like my own kids. She comes over and fusses over my health before looking for treats in my cupboards!*

Sra. Rosalia chuckles to herself when she remembers how much Joyce enjoyed the *hallacas* at Christmas. What did Yolí say about them? Sra. Rosalia asks herself. Yes, she said the *hallacas* reminded her of the Chinese tamales her family makes for the Dragon Boat Festival. But instead of cornmeal dough filled with meat, raisins and olives and wrapped in plantain leaves, the Chinese tamale is filled made with sweet rice mixed with meat, eggs and beans wrapped in banana leaves.

Joyce is closer to home than she thinks. Sra. Rosalia finishes her thought.

"*Dios te bendiga,*" Sra. Rosalia says a blessing over her *chinita* and returns her attention to her ironing. She has learned to hold the presence of God gently in her open hands.

Neighbors

EVANGELIN STANDS IN front of her stove with her back to her guests. All four burners are lit. The biggest pot boils her family's drinking water. In the next pot over, black beans slowly simmer over low heat. On the front two burners, one pan fries the first of many *empanadas*, and the other heats milk for *cafecitos*. Her hands are a blur, expertly moving over the pots and pans. Her attention is focused on the conversation behind her.

It is Monday night and Amelia and Joyce have stopped in and joined Enrique and the boys around the kitchen table. Enrique is goofing around with Raúl as Ángel watches and tries to join in.

"Ha! Ha!" Enrique's loud laugh booms. He pokes Raúl in the side and ruffles his newly buzzed head. Ángel leans on his dad and pokes him in the ribs tentatively.

"What's this?" Enrique feigns surprise and anger before grabbing Ángel around the waist, lifting him upside down onto his lap, and tickling him relentlessly as Ángel squirms with delight. Raúl jumps back into the game, and Enrique defends himself against his two sons. Amelia and Joyce laugh along with the family, enjoying the relaxed atmosphere at the end of a long day.

"Ah! Amelia!" Evangelin sighs loudly over her shoulder. "Are you feeling better?" Evangelin, a nurse, naturally slips into the role of caregiving for the *misioneras* that rent their small apartment below. Before Joyce and Amelia, Eva had lived there. She was a missionary with Little Steps for more than three years before she left a half year ago. Eva was the first to move into the *barrios* and live in the apartment. Amelia and Joyce have taken her place after their stay with their host families.

Evangelin was intimately familiar with Eva's allergies and is now concerned with Amelia's stomach bugs and Joyce's headaches. Evangelin, only a couple of years older than the girls, treats them as her younger sisters, watching out for these sojourners living so far away from their families. She has often wondered why they chose to live in the *barrios*. Even after the numerous times they have tried to explain, she still has only just begun to grasp the motivations behind their actions: to be God's presence, a friend, a companion.

"I'm feeling better," Amelia answers, smiling at the back of Evangelin's head. "The medicine the new doctor gave me has really helped. There's less blood in my stools, and I have more energy."

"This doctor, where did you find him?" Evangelin asks. She only trusts the *Cubanos*, the doctors working in the "oil for doctors" exchange program President Hugo Chavez set up with Cuba.

"Sra. Dara's son recommended him. Eduardo is interning at the hospital where he works." Amelia says, referencing the credibility of her host family's eldest son, whose dedication to his schoolwork has earned the respect of the whole *barrio*.

"Ah, Amelia, that's good." Evangelin is relieved to learn of the connection but does not stop worrying. "You really need to take care of yourself. Be careful of what you eat, and make sure you rest. You have a delicate system. It is not used to the diet here" She turns to look at Amelia. "Did you eat the soup I made you last night? Eva never had a problem with the food. With her, it was allergies. She was allergic to everything! And the number of pills she had to take and the number of doctors she visited. *Oof!*"

"Ángel, Raúl, have you washed your hands?" she gently slaps the small dirty hands reaching for the *empanadas*.

More fried cheese *empanadas* appear on the table and disappear just as fast as they are put down.

"How was your day, Evangelin?" Joyce asks when Evangelin finally sits down with her own plate of empanadas.

"Another long day, I worked all morning. Then I went to class all afternoon. I have to finish this project by Friday. Ah, Yolí, so much work! I don't see how I am going to finish everything!"

Evangelin pulls out her notebook from the backpack hanging from the dining room chair and flips it open. "See here? This is my schedule. Look at all these due dates! This Friday, my group has to make a presentation about the nervous system in front of the class. We have to draw diagrams and type out a report to turn in. My group is only meeting once before our presentation! *Oof!*" Evangelin passes around her neatly handwritten notebook pages to Amelia and Joyce. "Do you think I can go to the Little Steps office up in Las Colinas to type up the report? Will Thomas or Agnes or any of their kids be home to let me into the office? It shouldn't take too long. I have it already written out."

Once Evangelin is satisfied that her work has been thoroughly examined and admired, she changes the subject and asks Joyce, who has just returned from another visit to San Juanito to visit the Aguilas, "How are Sara and Adan?"

"They are doing all right. Scraping by somehow. Sara barely makes any money cleaning the apartment buildings in Bloque 13. Adan just finished his last mechanics class offered by Misión Vuelve Cara and is waiting for the government to issue his graduation certificate so he can apply for the grant to start a small appliance repair shop. But the government is slow. Adan is just trying to find odd jobs here and there to make enough money to get by," Joyce says.

"Ah, it's so hard. How are the kids? How is Daniel? Does he still have that cough? Did the medicine I gave Sara at the last *convivencia* help?"

"Yes, Daniel is doing better, but he is weak and gets sick often. Sara is always worried about him. He doesn't have a very good appetite."

"You hear that, Raúl?" Evangelin glances at her younger son, who is still picking at his first *empanada*.

"Raúl! Eat your *empanada*!" Enrique chides Raúl. "If you don't eat, you are never going to grow big and strong." Enrique punches Raúl playfully in the arm.

"¡Ya!" Raúl complains, looking down at his half-eaten *empanada* with disdain.

"Eat!" Enrique orders, as he slugs Raúl on the arm one last time.

Sr. Carlos

SR. CARLOS LIES on the cot as he has always lain these past eight years—stretched out on his back looking up at the rusty sheet metal. The dampness has saturated each thin layer of blanket covering his body and slowly but relentlessly creeps deeper and deeper into his aching joints. He works his jaws rhythmically as he chews a few leaves of *sanalotodo* to the sound of the rain, to the expanding and contracting of his lungs, to the sound of his heartbeat. His leathery hand slowly moves over the thin, worn blankets toward the edge of the bed until his fingertips feel the familiar warmth and smoothness of the staff he has carried most of his life. Painfully, he closes his arthritic fingers around the stick, his anchor.

In the next room, he hears the voices of his children and grandchildren.

"*¡Hija!*" Sr. Carlos coughs, clearing his lungs. "*¡Hija!*"

A slender girl, no older than 17, pokes her head through the curtain into his partitioned room with a baby propped on her hip. "*¿Sí, Papá?*"

"Bring me some water!"

The curtain falls back. The girl disappears behind it.

He waits.

"Bring me some water!" Sr. Carlos demands impatiently once more.

"*Lo siento*," the girl comes in apologetically with a cup of water, the baby still propped on her hip. "The *gringo* is here," she informs him.

The gringo has been coming around more regularly lately, Sr. Carlos thinks to himself. That tall skinny white man, he sits and listens, really listens. Leaning forward, attentive, as if he is seeking some answer to a question he does not yet know how to ask.

"Let him come in," he instructs.

"Sí," the girl again disappears behind the curtain.

Faint footsteps on the dirt floor. The curtain lifts one more time, and stays lifted, tied back by a rope.

Thomas hunches over and steps into the room.

"*Hola, Sr. Carlos*," Thomas greets the old man lying on the mattress with a smile.

"*Hola*," Sr. Carlos says.

Thomas sits down on the stool next to the bed.

"The rain is coming down hard today, isn't it?" Thomas asks as he lays his wet umbrella next to his feet. "How are you doing?"

"Ah, fine. Always the same. How are you?" Sr. Carlos replies with a toothless smile.

"Well," Thomas continues, "I just got back from a trip to the States. I was able to spend some time with my brother I told you about in Los Angeles. I also got a chance to see Chris. You remember Chris, don't you? He left Venezuela to get married. He remembers you and sends his greetings."

Why does he reveal so much about himself? Sr. Carlos wonders, stroking his staff. Doesn't he know that the more he shares, the more vulnerable he becomes? No, of course not. He is inexperienced in the ways of the spirits.

The girl comes in without the baby this time. Instead, she carries a tray of *cafecitos* and crackers. She hands a cup of coffee to the guest and places the crackers on a night table next to Sr. Carlos's head.

"*Bien provecho,*" Sr. Carlos invites the guest to drink and eat of his home's hospitality.

"*Gracias,*" Thomas says. He sips his *cafecito* politely and takes a couple of dry crackers to show his appreciation of Sr. Carlos's welcome.

Sr. Carlos watches Thomas as he drinks and eats his food. He smiles, pleased that his guest is satisfied with his hospitality.

"Sr. Carlos, is that girl your daughter?" Thomas asks to break the silence that has settled in the room.

"No," Sr. Carlos replies. "She is the wife of my third son, Oscar."

"Oh? I don't believe that I've met him. Is he at work?" Thomas inquires.

"No, he died," Sr. Carlos answers.

"What happened?" Thomas asks, shocked.

"He was shot, by someone who we thought was his friend."

Thomas waits for Sr. Carlos to continue.

How can he be so nosy without knowing anything about what's happening under his nose? Sr. Carlos wonders. He takes a deep breath and describes to his guests the violence of the *barrios,* the violence in his home.

"This was about a year ago, after the rains of last fall." The memory of the violence seeps back vividly into Sr. Carlos's memory: his son lying on the broken concrete outside, moaning and calling out for help, he not able to do anything but lie as he always lies on his cot.

"What happened? Was the guy caught?"

"Caught?" Sr. Carlos chuckles, "By whom? The cops don't come up here. The farthest they dare to venture is the bottom of these hills. His friend backstabbed him over a drug deal." He pauses. When he speaks again, his eyes narrow, "I have put a curse on this traitor's life."

Thomas unconsciously recoils from the old withered man lying on the cot, distancing himself from the unknown darkness. *A curse? What kind of curse?*

Sr. Carlos holds up his staff above his body and shakes it, rattling the talismans that dangle from one end. "I have ways to bring justice."

"How did you put the curse on the friend?" Thomas asks.

Sr. Carlos reaches over to his nightstand and gingerly opens a book, taking out a picture and passes it to Thomas.

"You see this picture?" Sr. Carlos asks.

Thomas sees two young men, both shirtless, with arms around each other laughing. They are standing on a mound of dirt next to the beginnings of a foundation to a new house. Two young men, at the height of their health and friendship.

"That is Oscar standing on the right. He and his friend were visiting my relatives in Maracay," Sr. Carlos arches his neck and strains to see the picture alongside Thomas. "That was the last time my son saw any of my relatives, the last time any of them saw him."

"This friend of his," Sr. Carlos stabs at the young lad with his thin arthritic index finger. "This friend of his shot him." Sr. Carlos spits on the floor and scowls in disgust.

For a second, Sr. Carlos is consumed with bitterness. Thomas waits patiently for him to continue. He waits as Sr. Carlos reaches back through time, revisiting memories as frayed as the thin blanket covering his frail body. When he speaks again, the lines on Sr. Carlos's eyes and mouth are somehow more deeply engraved with resolve. "I have put a curse on this *friend* through this picture."

Sr. Carlos looks at his guest and sees fear and sadness etched in his face. "What are you thinking?" he asks Thomas.

"Why revenge? Violence begets violence," Thomas ventures to reply. "Is it not enough that one young man has lost his life?"

Sr. Carlos takes a deep breath, drawing on all his patience before attempting to explain life's complexities, right and wrong, the give and take that keeps the world balanced.

"It is how the world works. You always have to pay for what you have done, what you want to do, what you hope to do," Sr. Carlos begins. "There are always consequences. Nothing happens in a vacuum. Everything is connected. Even my son's death, my sons' deaths."

"What happened to your other sons?" Thomas asks, with a look of confusion on his face.

"I have four sons. I had four sons. Three of them have been killed."

"I'm sorry to hear that," Thomas's eyes fill with sympathy. He pauses for a moment before tentatively asking, "How are your sons' deaths connected?"

"Fate connects them. Years ago, when I first began to understand the world, when I first started learning of the forces that propel the world forward, I had the opportunity to learn, to tap into and control some of these forces, to gain the power to communicate with the spirits, to make things happen. However, in order to access this power, I had to make a pact, to give something of value in exchange."

"What was that?"

"My sons."

"Your sons?"

"I made a pact with the most powerful of the spirits, whose name when uttered has the power to summon the winds—may all my sacrifices appease him and satisfy his will—a pact in which I gave him my sons, one every five years as a sacrifice in exchange for the powers," Sr. Carlos answers with traces of determination and bitterness. "I have one more son."

"But if Oscar's death were a sacrifice, then why the curse on his friend?"

"Action begets action. There are always consequences."

"But your sons…" Thomas asks exasperated, dismayed.

"Life does not end in this temporal world. They are and will continue to be…" Sr. Carlos finishes his explanation and stops speaking.

After a short silence, Thomas ventures, "I have a story. May I share it with you?"

"Of course," Sr. Carlos replies, always welcoming a distraction.

"This is a story from the Bible, a similar story to yours. Perhaps you have already read or heard this story. This story is set in the time of the Judges, before the Israelites asked God for a king to rule over them,"

Thomas continues, "In the story, a warrior named Jephthah in the tribe of Israel was fighting against a people called the Ammonites. He vowed to the Lord that if the Lord granted him victory, he would sacrifice, as a burnt offering, the first thing that came out of his house to greet him when he returned in triumph. Jephthah went into battle, and the Lord granted him victory.

"When he returned home, his only child, his daughter, Mizpah, ran out to greet him. Jephthah was stricken with grief at the prospect of losing his child, but he could not go back on his vow. He sacrificed his virgin daughter, his only child, to keep his vow to the Lord," Thomas finishes his story and waits to hear Sr. Carlos's reaction.

"Yes, the story is similar," Sr. Carlos concludes. "This story is a good illustration of life."

"But you know what is interesting?" Thomas interjects. "It says in the story that the Spirit of the Lord was already upon him before he made the vow. The land he was fighting over, it was already given to the tribe of Israel when they came out of Egypt.

"It was already given to the tribe of Israel by the Lord," Thomas emphasizes. "The Bible said Jephthah had recounted this history to the king of the Ammonites even before going into battle, by claiming the Israelites' rightful ownership of the land and attempting to dissuade the king from unjust aggression."

Thomas pauses.

Sr. Carlos watches Thomas looking curiously about the room, at the talismans and dried herbs hanging from the walls and ceiling and smelling the smoky incense drifting heavily over his reed-thin body lying there on the cot.

"I wonder," Thomas speaks, "What if God was already intending to grant Jephthah victory before Jephthah made his vow?"

Minutes pass. The question hangs in the air, unanswered.

"That is a good story, Thomas," Sr. Carlos says, amused. "I like your stories, I like sharing stories with you." He smiles at his young guest, who is not afraid to venture into the world of spirits and the supernatural. *But he has much to learn, so innocent and idealistic,* Sr. Carlos thinks. *Reality is so much harsher than what the human soul desires.*

Sr. Carlos is tired. The visit, though pleasant, has drained his energy. "Let's talk more about this next time you visit," he says. He makes slight movements to show his weariness. "When will you come again?"

"Next week," Thomas says. He sets down his cup on the small nightstand next to Sr. Carlos's head and stands to leave.

After the visitor has left, Sr. Carlos lies on his cot and caresses the smooth surface of his staff with his fingers, drawing strength from his anchor.

#

Thomas takes a sip of his tea and looks out his window over the *barrios*. He watches the urban fireflies, the naked light bulbs strung along paths of *callejones* and over doorways. *Mr. Carlos is there, lying in his cot, somewhere down there,* he thinks.

He returns his gaze to the computer screen and reads the prayer letter he has started, a letter to be sent to friends and family scattered around the world, friends and family who have faithfully supported him throughout his twenty-five years in ministry among the urban poor.

"Mr. Carlos, as we call him, is an elderly man steeped in witchcraft and Spiritism," he reads.

He has been bedridden for eight years due to a problem with his nervous system. With his rich, brown skin, white beard and pencil-thin body, you feel like you are in Mother Theresa's home for the destitute and dying. Though not dying, I would not say that Mr. Carlos is really living either. Mr.

Carlos is captive to witchcraft, through which he is avenging the murder of his 20-year-old son.

He has told me that one of his son's killers will be eliminated. I, in turn, am challenging him to renounce vengeance and follow Christ. It's an interesting relationship we've developed."

Family Lunch

EIGHT-YEAR-OLD Matt Reed kicks the soccer ball against the patio wall, adding another mark on the stucco. Peanut, the family's four-legged mutt, dances excitedly around Matt's feet, wagging her tail. *Thump! Thump! Thump!* The explosions on the wall accompany the beats of raggaeton blasting from stereos and the dog barks that fill the early afternoon air.

Matt fakes a pass to his phantom teammate, juggles the ball between his feet, aims at a blank space on the wall, and kicks hard. *Thump!*

" G-o-o-a-al! Goal! Venezuela's Number 8, Matt Reed, scores!!" Matt narrates to the packed stadium in his mind. "Let's see that play again. What a beautiful textbook shot! Look how the ball arches in the air, barely grazing Oliver Kahn's finger tips. What a shot! Matt Reed ties the game for his team, one–one. With only one minute left on the clock, it looks like we will be going into overtime..."

"Matt!" his mom Agnes calls from inside the house.

"¡*Ya va*! Hold your horses, I'm coming!" Matt replies, trying to hold off the end of the game for a few more seconds.

"Matt! Come inside for lunch!" Agnes's voice finally pierces through the roaring crowd and brings Matt back to Las Colinas, his home, his *barrio* in Caracas.

"All right, all right!" Matt reluctantly gives the ball a final kick before heading inside.

His two older sisters, Sharon, and Anna, emerge from their rooms, dragging their feet.

"Anna, can you set the table?" Agnes asks her middle child.

"Yeah, sure," Anna answers.

Sharon, meanwhile, walks over to the stove where Thomas is forming *arepas* out of cornmeal batter with his hands.

"Hi, Dad," she pecks her dad's cheek and peers over his shoulder to assess the progress of the *arepas* sizzling in the cast iron frying pan Agnes brought from the States. She goes over to the fridge and takes out the margarine, shredded cheese, and leftover black beans from last night to fill the *arepas*.

"Don't we have any ham?" she asks her mom accusingly.

"No, we don't," Agnes answers, distracted. Her attention is focused on Matt's hands. "Did you wash your hands?"

"*Sí*," Matt mumbles.

"Did you use soap?"

"Ah, Mom!" Matt protests as he drags himself to the kitchen sink.

"Not in the kitchen sink! The bathroom!"

At the stove, Thomas flips the last of the fried *arepas* onto the plate and carries them over to the table. He places them down among the fillings and condiments. Sharon's and Anna's hands simultaneously reach in to grab the piping hot *arepas*.

Matt returns to the table after a quick trip to the bathroom.

"I don't want *arepas* again," he whines. "Can I have oatmeal?"

Agnes looks at her youngest. "Yes, you can get it yourself."

Matt gets up from his chair and goes to the kitchen, taking his time pulling out the container of oatmeal and the carton of milk. He pours the oatmeal and the milk into a bowl and adds heaping spoonfuls of sugar on top.

Everyone is once again sitting at the table. The *arepas* are sliced open. Gold steam rises out of the soft, moist centers. Layers of margarine, cheese and beans are piled on. The juices of the black beans and margarine drip down fingers and hands over plates and are licked off by greedy tongues. The *arepas* disappear into hungry stomachs.

"Can Samantha come over tomorrow?" Anna asks. "We want to work on the dance routine for the church."

"Can Roberto come over too?" Matt pipes in, excited at the prospect of having a real teammate to play soccer with.

"Your dad and I will be out all day. No one will be able to go meet them at the Redoma or take them home," Agnes answers pragmatically.

"They could come up with us after school," Anna responds with a ready answer. "And we could ask their dad to pick them up afterward. They just bought a car!"

Agnes looks over at her husband, who is concentrating on eating his *arepa*. He seems to be oblivious to the possible scenarios that plague her. Her blond children stand out among the dark haired Venezuelans, easy targets for robbers.

Even worse, Agnes thinks to herself, *they could catch a stray bullet*. She knows Thomas would never be careless with their children. She can trust him. But at times, he takes risks she would not dream of, like moving to one of the most dangerous *barrios* in Caracas for their ministry as if the neighborhoods of East L.A. were not dangerous enough.

"Check with their parents, only if their parents are okay with it," Agnes finally relents.

Matt bolts off his seat and runs for the phone.

"After lunch, Matt!" Agnes calls after him.

Matt returns to the table, dejected.

"Dad, can we play a game of backgammon after lunch?" Matt turns his attention to the next best thing at the moment.

Thomas looks at his son and smiles. "One game."

"I'm done. Can I go? I need to finish my homework," Sharon asks.

"What are you working on?" Thomas asks, looking over at his eldest who is dressed in the latest *barrio* style of a tight T-shirt, blue jeans, chintzy earrings and bangles.

"Chemistry," Sharon answers with a look of disgust.

"How are you doing?"

"It's hard. I don't know why we have to learn this stuff." Sharon picks up her plate and heads to the sink, leaving the conversation behind.

Back at the table, Anna tells Matt to close his mouth when he chews. "That's soooo disgusting, Matt!"

Matt smacks his lips and exaggerates his chewing all the more, basking in the attention he solicits whenever he irritates his sisters.

"Mom! Tell him to chew with his mouth closed!"

"Matt!"

All the *arepas* have disappeared from the plate, leaving only smears of grease. The leftover beans and cheese are rewrapped and placed back into the fridge, and the plates are cleared away.

Anna stands over the kitchen sink. It is her turn to do the dishes. Agnes cleans the kitchen counter. Matt and Thomas move over to the couch with the backgammon board between them.

Matt is getting better at the game, Thomas notes. Both Thomas and Matt take pride in the fact.

"Yes!" Matt shouts in triumph as he knocks Thomas's red pieces back to the beginning.

Peanut wags her tail, exulting in the excitement of her little master before running outside, barking at the passing jeeps below.

Morning Walk

AGNES WALKS DOWN the hill. The sun is just starting to come up. The hills across the valley glow with the first rays of light. The grass is freshly kissed by the morning dew. Peanut pulls on her leash, leading Agnes down the steep descent from Las Colinas to the baseball field for their morning jog. They walk by the *ranchitos* lining the road.

One *ranchito* halfway down the hill has undergone a transformation in the past few weeks. One of the shaky cardboard plywood walls has been replaced by a half-finished wall of gray cinder blocks. Agnes hopes more blocks are on their way to finish the rest of the wall, that it will not stand half-finished like so many homes in the *barrios*, deteriorating day by day as the hapless owners wait months on end for the next windfall of cash to buy the next batch of cinder blocks.

Mario Sanchez walks up the hill toward Agnes, carrying his daily supply of coffee to sell at the Redoma. Mario knows Agnes well. Agnes and her husband Thomas have been coming by their *ranchito* for a couple of years now, asking after them and their five, now six, young boys. He has shared with them bits and pieces of his past, his time in prison, his conversion and his marriage, and he has allowed them to witness his current state of existence.

Most recently, Agnes and Thomas have tried to help when the neighbors shut off the water that is piped in bimonthly to their *ranchito*. The neighbors took such a drastic measure in order to pressure Mario's family to stop burning their trash in the road, but the attempt only angered them.

Agnes and Thomas have tried to act as a go-between but to no avail. After countless formal and informal meetings, they still have to store water in rusty oil barrels inside their home, and their neighbors still have to smell the acid black smoke blanketing their *barrio* every morning and evening.

Still, Agnes and Thomas continue to care, continue to pray for them, continue to offer their friendship.

"*Hola*, Mario. Are you going off to work?

"How's your family, Mario? How's your youngest, Alfonzo? Have the burns on his arm and back healed?

"Is your wife home? I want to check in with her about your children's IDs. They would be able to get more services if they had them.

"Have a good day, Mario."

Mario returns Agnes's greetings and answers her questions politely. *She is a nice lady*, he thinks to himself. He hopes his wife will not give Agnes too much grief if she stops by. He knows how much she hates other people butting into her business. She tries hard to be a good wife, a good mother. But he also knows how hard it is when you are a stranger without any familial ties in the community, when you have no money, when the world never seems to give you a break.

Mario continues up the hill. He hopes he will be coming down the hill in a few hours with an empty coffee thermos and enough *bolívares* to buy bread, and maybe, just maybe, an 8 oz brown bottle of Polar beer to take the edge off of what always is a long day.

Agnes stops and follows Mario with her eyes. She watches Mario climb the hill, his head bent low. It has been four years since she and Thomas moved with their three kids into the *barrio* on top of the hill. Like Mario's dragging footsteps, the years have passed laboriously. The struggles of the first years—learning the language, learning to shop at the market, finding schools for the kids, befriending strangers—are still daunting, requiring so much time, effort, and assistance.

For her, ministry has been just as slow. The methods and accomplishments they read about concerning other ministries seem so farfetched, idealistic. *How come no one ever writes anything about the first years of struggle, where nothing seems to get accomplished?* Agnes often wonders. *Relationships start and peter out. Ministry projects falter before they even start.*

Yet as Agnes watches Mario climb the hill, she also sees, however faintly, the hand of God in all of this seemingly meaningless passing of days. In the two years she and Thomas have befriended Mario and his family, she knows that God has been ministering to both Mario's family and hers. The call to surrender to the mystery of God's will and patiently wait for God to unveil his plans is the only call she feels capable of heeding.

Agnes turns back toward the baseball field. Peanut wags her tail and urges Agnes on.

One step at a time, Agnes breathes out the tension and anxiety in the pit of her stomach. One step at a time, she breathes in the fresh morning air.

Saturday Morning Chores

THE JEEPS FLY by, packed with passengers. They weave their way down the hill to the Redoma, where, on Saturday mornings, vendors line the streets with fresh produce all the way to the metro station, Ruiz Pineda, six blocks away.

Joyce has been standing at the top of the *callejon* for at least ten minutes, trying to wave down a jeep and save herself the walk down to the Redoma. Having seen at least eight jeeps packed full of passengers go by, she gives up hope of catching one. She picks up her empty backpack and follows after the jeeps down the hill.

She is running late. Usually, she is out of the apartment by 8 a.m. to finish her weekly market trip by 11, so she can beat the crowd waiting for the jeeps coming back up the hill.

Amelia is still asleep, but will probably wake up soon to start cleaning the apartment.

The girls have an arrangement of splitting up the chores. They have worked it out over the months they have lived together. Joyce likes shopping, picking out the freshest and ripest mangos and haggling with the vendors over the price of *platanos*. Amelia loves tidying up the apartment and mopping the concrete floor with hot buckets of soapy pine-scented Pinesol.

"The other scents, Green Apple, Wild Sparkling or this newest, White Flower Blast, they just don't smell as clean," Amelia told Joyce when she brought home the offending bottle of White Flower Blast scented Pinesol a couple months back.

Joyce does not see dust. She appreciates the absence of it after the fact and likes the feel of a clean and tidy room - also after the fact.

Amelia gets a headache trying to figure out how much things should cost. She hates the throngs of shoppers jostling through the narrow aisles packed streets and sidewalks, weaving past hawkers of toothpaste and rat poison under the harsh sun as she tries to make her way through the open market. She also dislikes the attention she gets as a *gringa*, especially from the men.

As a *chinita*, Joyce somehow blends in better and does not draw the same kind of unwanted attention. If she gets asked anything at all, it is whether she works at a Chinese restaurant or if she knows how to make *arroz chino*.

So Joyce does the grocery shopping, working off of the list of items she and Amelia jot down in the spiral notebook on top of the fridge during the week. And Amelia does the cleaning in the solitude of an empty apartment after Joyce leaves for the market. It is a good arrangement.

A car honks behind Joyce. Without looking back, she moves closer to the edge of the rain gutter to get out of the way.

"*¡Hola, Yoli!*" the driver sticks his head out of the car window and hollers her adopted Venezuelan name.

"*Hola, Ramón. ¿Cómo estás?*" Joyce replies, recognizing her neighbor the *taxista*.

"*Bien, bien.* Are you heading down to the market? Want a ride?"

"*¡Por supuesto!*" surprised but delighted, she accepts the offer.

Joyce walks around the back of the 40-year old jalopy, opens the passenger door and sits down on the torn vinyl upholstered seat. She reaches automatically for the seatbelt before realizing, once again, its absence.

"Where are you going?" Joyce asks.

"I'm going to go visit my mom in Los Telares."

"How is she doing?" Joyce asks, remembering how dejected Ramón had seemed the last time she saw him sitting listlessly in front of his house.

"All right. My sister has been staying with my mother since she left the hospital."

"Is she able to move around much?"

"*Sí.* She's been much better this last week, though she is still quite weak."

"What does the doctor say?"

"She'll have to watch her diet, exercise more, and not work so much – the same stuff she's heard for years now."

They continue making small talk as the jalopy winds its way down to the bottom of the hill.

The car stops in front of the *farmacia* located outside the Redoma where a line of women stand outside the building waiting for their turn to buy government-subsidized powdered milk. It is delivered at irregular intervals to pharmacies throughout the year as part of a health initiative. The women worriedly strain their necks to see whether the supply will last until their turn. Powdered milk is twice as expensive in the open market.

"*Bueno, gracias Ramón. Saluda a tu mamá para mí.*" Joyce steps out of the jalopy, and slams the door. She double checks to make sure the door is shut all the way.

"*¡A la orden!* I will tell *mi mamá* you said, 'Hi!'" Joyce's neighbor waves. The tail pipe of the jalopy blows out a heavy cloud of black exhaust as it pulls away from the curb to merge back into bumper-to-bumper traffic meandering through the Saturday market crowd.

Joyce walks past the line of women waiting outside the *farmacia* and heads towards the metro station. Her plan is to start at the far end of the Saturday street market and make her way back through the food market in the Redoma and get in line for the jeep back by the *farmacia* where Ramón dropped her off.

She stops first at the government food co-op. Everything is Bs. 2,000 a kilo. She gets in line behind the other shoppers and works her way around the long tables in the middle of the tent, picking out different vegetables and putting them into plastic bags. When she gets around the tables, she again waits her turn to weigh and pay for the produce she has selected. The potatoes, carrots, zucchini, tomatoes and onions she has picked cost only Bs. 5,000.

$2.50, not bad, Joyce does the quick conversion in her mind.

She loads her backpack with the potatoes on the bottom and tomatoes on top and continues down the street.

She stops at a booth where a vendor is selling homemade frozen juice concentrate. They are a bit pricy at Bs. 4,000 for each pack, but these juice concentrates have come in handy whenever she and Amelia have visitors. She asks for a *mora* and a *guanavana*. Sra. Rosalia, told her once that *guanavana* juice gave people strange dreams. But of the exotic tropical fruits she has been introduced to so far, *guanavana* has been her favorite. It has just the right amount of sweetness to balance its tangy flavor and is more than refreshing on hot, humid afternoons.

By the time she makes her way to the Redoma, her backpack is already packed with fresh fruits and vegetables, a bag of coffee, and a bag of powdered milk – paid for at market price. She carries half a tray of eggs in one hand, not wanting to break them by putting them in her backpack. The price of eggs has gone up as well, from Bs. 3,200 to Bs. 3,500.

The Venezuelan *bolívar* buys less and less with each passing day. Joyce realizes again how fortunate she is to have the financial support she receives from friends and family back home in the States. The U.S. dollars deposited into a U.S. bank account never depreciate against the *bolívar,* and the money is available for her to withdraw whenever she needs it. As tight as her budget is, she has yet to worry about not having enough money to buy market priced powdered milk.

She hurriedly passes the meat and chicken stalls reeking of wet chicken feathers and covered with flies. She ignores, with a mixture of annoyance and pleasure, the friendly cat-calls from the boys behind the elevated glass cases filled with various cuts of beef, pork and chicken. She makes her way towards a vegetable stall piled high with tubers, squashes and leafy greens.

"*Hola Samuel. ¿Cómo estás?* Do you have any fresh basil today?"

"*Por supuesto.*"

"I'd like to have a bunch of that, and give me a kilo of *hoyama* as well. *Gracias.*"

"*A la orden,*" Samuel responds automatically.

Samuel has had his vegetable stand for about six months now. Thomas and Agnes assisted him in getting his stand in the Redoma, and Joyce always tries to buy something from him on market day.

Both of Joyce's hands are full now. But before getting in line for the jeeps, she has to make one more stop at the *panadería*. At the bakery, she buys three loaves of *campesino* bread for the *cafecitos* and a tub of margarine for the *arepas*.

Joyce has learned that arepas, the corn cakes Venezuelans have at almost every meal, just do not taste quite as good without margarine no matter what fillings you stuff them with. After paying, she packs the margarine in the last few cubic centimeters of free space in her backpack, and manages to hook her pinky through the thin plastic bag holding the bread. Fully loaded down with food and out of *bolívares*, Joyce joins the line for the jeeps heading up the hill.

The line is relatively short, about two jeeps full of passengers are lined up in front of her. Women, with mountainous black plastic bags of groceries filled with yucca and black beans, soon line up behind her, weary from shopping all morning.

The BonIce man in a blue and purple penguin jumpsuit carries his ice cooler up and down the line selling frozen water pops for Bs. 300. With both hands full and not much longer to wait, Joyce shakes her head when the BonIce man nods at her.

After a few minutes, a yellow jeep rumbles to the front of the line. Joyce counts herself twelfth in line. She will be the last passenger to squeeze into the jeep. She steps off the curb and moves forward in unison with eleven other passengers. Two people get in next to the driver up front and the other ten, including Joyce, move to the rear of the jeep to climb into the extended cab—one laden passenger at a time.

The first passengers situate themselves on either side of door so they will not need to climb over grocery bags that will soon cover the floor. Joyce is last to get in. She squeezes herself into the remaining few centimeters of the bench between two rotund women, one of whom carries a baby on her lap. Joyce braces herself for the bumpy, twisty, uphill ride.

The jeep slowly makes its way up the hill, jostling around sharp turns and laboring up steep inclines. It passes the pedestrians lumbering along the edge of the road. The sweaty bodies packed into the back of the jeep mash against each other for an eternity before the jeep finally approaches the entrance of Joyce's *callejon*.

"*¡En la parada!*" Joyce shouts half-heartedly for the driver to stop. She is self-conscious of her mispronunciation. The "rada" always trips her tongue up. She is conscious of all the other passengers' shameless stares bearing down on the *chinita* who cannot seem to pronounce the simplest of commands.

The jeep comes to a halt, right in front of her *callejon*. Joyce manages to find a few inches of space on the jeep's cab floor among the bags of groceries to place her feet and climbs cautiously out of the jeep.

Fresh air! Joyce breathes out a sigh of relief.

\#

"*¡Hola! ¿Cómo estás?*" Joyce balances the bags of groceries carefully as she pauses to greet Evangelin on the steps leading down to her apartment. She leans toward her to exchange a greeting kiss.

"*Bien.* How was the market?"

"Good. I'm exhausted though! What are you up to today?"

"When I am done cleaning, we are going to visit Enrique's mom."

"Agnes mentioned to me yesterday that she was planning on stopping by your place tonight," Joyce passes on the message from her teammate.

"We'll probably be here. The visit shouldn't take long."

"*Bueno*. I'll see you later."

"Bueno. Chao."

"*¡Hola, Yoli!*" Ángel calls out, poking out his head from behind the curtains of a window. "Can I come down and play cards?"

"Amelia's cleaning right now, but maybe later when you guys get back from your grandma's."

"Ok. *¡Chao!*" Ángel's head disappears as quickly as it appeared, happily anticipating spending time with Joyce and Amelia in the evening.

Joyce unlocks her door, gingerly stepping on the barely dry concrete floor. She sets the groceries down on the table and sits herself down by the window for a short rest.

Church

THE PADRE SITS down in the chair on the stage of the sanctuary. He smiles at his congregation.

"God be with you."

"And also with you," his people respond.

"It is good to see so many of you here today." The Padre scans the rows filled with families. "Is there anyone here for the first time?"

Two women in the back stand up. "This is my cousin, Graciela, visiting from Valencia."

"*Bienviendos*, my sister from Valencia. We are glad you are here with us today," the Padre says with genuine warmth. The woman beams back at the Padre.

A few others stand and introduce themselves and their guests. After a pause, the Padre leans back in his chair and opens his Bible.

"Earlier, Brother Juan read the parable of the good Samaritan. In the parable, a man was robbed. Who stopped to help him?"

"Not the Levite or the priest, but a Samaritan," he answers after a brief pause.

The Padre looks at the faces of his congregation. He has been at this parish for over twenty-five years, and these are his people. His flock has grown over the years despite the austere building. The sanctuary is empty of statues of saints and stain glass windows. In their places are the colorful banners made by the youth group. Instead of an ornate façade, a plain wooden cross. Instead of pews, metal fold-up chairs. He has tried to keep his church simple, stretching the diocese's funds to finance community programs rather than decor, hoping the simplicity would unclutter the minds of his parishioners so the core message of an intimate and personal relationship with God could be heard.

"This Samaritan was probably a traveler himself, anxious to get to his destination quickly. The road to Jericho was not a safe one. Yet, the Samaritan stopped to help a stranger. Did he think to himself that someone else will probably stop to help? That the Romans who sporadically patrol the roads would take care of this man?" The Padre pauses after each question to give his audience a moment to reflect.

Then he continues, "These thoughts probably crossed his mind. But there was something in him that propelled him to stop and help this stranger."

When the Padre feels that sufficient time has passed for each person in the audience to identify with the Samaritan, he speaks to the reality his parish lives in today.

"In our country, we have government programs like Misión Robinson that give adults an opportunity to learn to read and write, Comité de Salud, the Cuban doctors, the food programs. They are there to help those in need, the sick, the poor. Yet in and of themselves, these programs lack moral fiber because they are structures and shells for people in the community to fill and enrich.

"We need to take part in the communities we live in, to add the moral fiber with the insight of grace and love we have from God and the church community, to share the Christ we know with our neighbors. It is not enough for us to tell people what they need to be; we need to visit the sick, share with the poor."

He looks over at Joyce and Amelia sitting among the parishioners. He notices that they have, once again, brought Ángel with them. Ángel is sitting as still and as attentive as the widows in the front row.

"Here in our corner of Caracas, we have a group of foreigners who have chosen to live out the life of the Good Samaritan."

The eyes of the parishioners follow the gaze of the Padre.

"These brothers and sisters, they have chosen to live up in the *barrios* among the poorest of the poor, to visit with their neighbors and to be a part of their lives."

The Padre smiles in Joyce and Amelia's direction, sojourners like himself who came from a different country to follow the call of God, he from Cuba and they from the United States. "Please stand up, Amelia, Yolí!" he instructs.

The girls stand, embarrassed by the praise and attention.

The Padre turns back to the rest of the congregation and addresses them. "Like them, we are also called to be a part of our communities, though we don't have to travel as far. We should not keep to ourselves, only speaking with those who are familiar to us, who talk like us, who dress like us. How else will God answer our prayers for our community?

"If you say there is too much sickness in these neighborhoods, I say to you, be a part of Comité de Salud, visit the sick.

"If you complain that there are too many kids running around hungry, volunteer to cook food for the food program.

"If you protest the violence that plagues our neighborhoods, introduce yourself to those neighbors whom you walk by every morning, avoiding eye contact.

"My brothers and sisters, our faith in God is not a faith to receive what we ask for, but a faith to surrender and participate in His will.

"Let us go out and love one another, love our neighbors in the way the scripture illustrates for us in the story of the Good Samaritan."

The Padre closes the Bible on his lap and bows his head in prayer.

Joyce, Amelia and Ángel, along with the rest of the congregation, also bow their heads.

#

Joyce and Amelia walk out of the cool darkness of the building and into the midday Sunday sun with Ángel skipping between them. They pause every few steps to greet and exchange pleasantries with familiar faces.

"Hola, Sra. Julia."

"Dios bendiga."

"¿Cómo están?"

"Saluda a tu mamá para nosotros."

"Ve en paz."

Though neither Joyce nor Amelia is Catholic, the Padre and his congregation have been a sanctuary in the midst of dogmatic, charismatic evangelicals and nominal high-holiday Catholics. The Padre is a role model and mentor, for them and for their team. The masses he gives speak of grace, of living out that grace in the day-to-day. These messages resonate with their own sense of calling that has drawn them to join the team, to live in the *barrios* of Caracas.

They are humbled. They did not realize that the Padre was going to prop them up as examples to the rest of the congregation.

As they make their way from the church next to the Redoma to the line for the jeeps to go back up the hill, Joyce and Amelia whisper under their breath a prayer for grace and perseverance. That they may find motivation and energy for the mundane day-to-day activities that seem so distant from the glamorous missionary projects and accomplishments they read about. That God's love, in its mysterious way, will be communicated to each person whose paths they cross.

"Amelia, why did the Padre ask you and Joyce to stand up?" Ángel asks.

"Because he thought what we do in the *barrios* is similar to what the Good Samaritan did in the story," Amelia answers.

"Why?"

"Well, what do you think?"

"Because you spend time with people?"

"Maybe."

"Because you came to live in the *barrios* with strangers?"

"Maybe."

A Visit

JOYCE WALKS BEHIND Amelia and Thomas up the uneven dirt steps into San Miguel, the *barrio* above Las Colinas. San Miguel, a relatively new *barrio*, barely ten years old, is still predominantly populated with recent migrants from the countryside seeking a better opportunity in the city. *Ranchitos* lining the *callejones* overflow with extended families struggling to scrape by in the informal economy of sewing shoes, selling candy, repairing broken cars and refrigerators.

Their first stop is at Gladys's. At last count, the plywood *ranchito* provides covering for more than twenty adults and children, a few dogs and cats and a handful of hens and birds.

"¡Hola!" The three enter the living space of the family. Exchanges of kisses are given from the oldest lounging on the sofa to the youngest resting contently in the arms of his mother. Mamá Rosa sends one of the kids who are peeking at the visitors from behind her skirt to find Gladys and shoos a few others off of the mismatched chairs scattered around the room. She pushes the chairs up against a wall and invites the guests to sit.

The visitors take their seats and wait. Visits to this family are a staple in the Thursday afternoon routine of the team. However, ever since Eva left six months ago to marry and start a family back in the States, the relational link with the family has been strained. Eva had made this family a priority in her ministry. She had spent hours upon hours sitting with Gladys swapping stories and sharing laughter. The void she left is still palpable. Gladys, the eldest daughter of Mamá Rosa, had a special bond with Eva that took years to cultivate. Eva's departure introduced a new element of loss. To ask Gladys's family to open their home up once again to strangers, to open their hearts to new friendships, is asking them to open their hearts up to loss. Both the visitors and the hosts are tentative as they try to navigate this new relationship.

"Gladys is sick. She's in her room. She said to invite them back," a little boy tells his grandmother.

The visitors stand and follow the boy past the chickens pecking at the crumbs on the kitchen floor and the partitioned rooms that house the extended family to Gladys's room.

Gladys is lying on her bed braiding her daughter's hair. She leans forward and greets her guests with the customary kisses. Gladys, the backbone of her family with her loud voice and even louder laugh, is spiritually strong even when she is physically weak. She shifts toward the wall to make space on her bed for her guests to sit as there is no space for more than two small stools on the floor. Amelia takes her seat on the bed while Thomas and Joyce sit down on the stools.

"How are you feeling?"

"I'm doing okay. The new meds the doctor gave me make me feel a little bit better. But the medicine is really expensive. My husband is picking up another job to help pay for it." Gladys begins to recount all the various hoops she has had to jump through to find the right doctors and the right prescriptions.

"That's tough. Where is he working?"

"At the theme park on the other side of the city. He works on the operating machines of the rides. He's great at that kind of stuff," Gladys pauses before venturing to ask after her friend. "How is Eva?"

"We just got an email from her. She's doing well. She and her husband are living with some friends until they find their own place. Since their wedding, Eva has found a job helping people apply for jobs. Her husband is having a harder time securing one. He's just trying to get accustomed to the U.S." Amelia racks her brain to remember all the contents of the last email update from Eva. "She says hi and wants me to tell you that she misses you."

"Sí, I miss her, too. But I'm glad she is married and is making a home for herself. She is always in my heart. Look, I keep the book she gave me under my pillow," Gladys pulls out a battered copy of Bible stories and lovingly touches the cover of the book. "God knows what he is doing," Gladys says, more to comfort herself than her guests.

Amelia reaches over and lays a hand on Gladys, silently praying for the same.

The temporal nature of missions work, the comings and goings of interns and lifelong missionaries alike, is hard on the team. But, for them, the uprooting is an innate part of the missionary lifestyle. How could they reach across the pain left by the loss of a friend and ask Gladys to once again risk losing another? Yet, Gladys is already opening up to them. Her ability to love is more resilient than her fear of loss. At least that is what Amelia and the rest of team are praying for. And even more, they pray that something of God's presence would somehow find eternal residence in Gladys's heart through these friendships.

After chatting a bit longer with Gladys, the visitors leave her to rest. They are ushered back into the living room to be with the rest of the family. Adults and kids stream in and out, each time stopping to greet each person in the room.

The guests sit respectfully in their chairs through the minutes of awkward silence that is a part of most visits. They allow time for their hosts to adjust to their guests and put aside their daily chores of cleaning, cooking, and minding the children. The patchy concrete floors need constant sweeping; the dishes never stop piling up in the overflowing sink; the kids demand constant feeding, changing, scolding and cooing.

Joyce finally makes eye contact with Zuli, who at the moment is breastfeeding her one-year-old baby girl.

Joyce smiles.

Zuli smiles back.

"*Cómo estás?*" Joyce takes a stab at starting conversation.

"Bien."

The conversation ends as Zoli returns her gaze to her child in her arms.

Time passes.

The guests listen to the reggaeton blasting from the stereos at full volume less than two feet away, patiently waiting for an opportunity to start a conversation.

The kids, the brave ones at first, respond to Amelia's offer to play with them outside. They follow Amelia out into the bare and hard-packed dirt courtyard. Amelia asks the kids if they know any songs they would like to sing. They vie for Amelia's attention, screaming at the top of their lungs the name of the songs they know, songs Eva taught them.

Under the blue skies of Caracas, on the steep face of a hill, in the bend of a road behind the planks of wood held together by rusty nails, Amelia begins to sing a song she has just learned, one so dear to the kids.

Pio pio pio
Dicen los pollitos
Cuando tienen hambre
Cuando tienen frio

La Gallina busca
El maiz y el trigo
Les da la comida
Y les presta abrigo

Pio, Pio, Pio
Said the baby chicks
When they are hungry
When they are cold

The hen looks
For corn and flour
She gives them food
She keeps them warm

The children flock around Amelia like a brood gathered around a mother hen. Amelia picks up the youngest of those tugging on the corner of her skirt, a two-year-old girl with dirt-streaked chubby cheeks and a matted mess of curls that bob every which way. Amelia swings her around and carries her on her hip as she dances with the rest of the swaying and jumping kids.

Inside, Thomas and Joyce strike up a conversation with Suyeli. Suyeli, the fourth daughter of Mamá Rosa, strokes the tousled hair of her baby boy on her lap as she responds to Joyce's question about her husband.

"My husband and I were so in love. He was so good to me. So much *cariño*. We met when we were little, playing together all the time with the other neighborhood kids. He would bring me flowers every time he came by, mostly picked from the hillside. It was so sweet! After we married, he moved in with us."

Suyeli pauses. As swiftly as the afternoon storm clouds blot out the sun, a shadow crosses Suyeli's face, erasing her dreamy smile of memories. "I was pregnant with this one, standing next to him, right outside the door where Amelia is dancing. A rival gang member rode by on a motorcycle, pulled out a pistol and shot him in the stomach. The baby turned in mine. I couldn't stop screaming."

Joyce does not know what to say, taken aback by the candidness of the story and the violence that will forever traumatize this young mother sitting in front of her. She knows, statistically, that every family living in these parts of Caracas has experienced the loss of a family member or loved one through violence. After each murder, the story burns through the *barrios* like brush fire.

"Did you hear that Juan got shot while riding up the hill in a jeep? He got caught in a gun fight between the robbers and the police and took a bullet in the neck."

"Simon was stabbed walking home from work last night. He shouldn't have resisted. He didn't have very much money anyway."

"Maria was robbed on her way to the market. She shouldn't have gone down the hill by herself so early in the morning."

The stories become longer, embellished with unquestionably real details from the Luises in the streets and the Alfredos at the *abastos*. The wrinkles of concern etch deeper into the faces of mothers, and the knuckles on the fists of fathers become whiter. The violence of the *barrios* instills a constant tension in the muscles of adults and children alike, only kept at bay by a quick laugh and a resolute joy found in people's spirits when friends gather and music plays.

Suyeli's account adds more Polaroids to the accumulating images of the *barrios* swimming inside Joyce's head. Images of Suyeli standing beside her husband... belly full and round... an unshaven man with a bulge under his jacket... a gun flashing under the afternoon sun... a look of shock and fear on the face of Suyeli... the wordless scream of her husband... a crumpled body on the ground... a pool of blood spreading and mixing with the dirt... the smell of exhaust from the motorcycle speeding away.

"A revenge for a slight at a bar six months prior... Who can remember what the slight was?... Here's a picture taken at our wedding."

Joyce listens, sympathizes. She holds a faded picture of a young couple in her hands. Suyeli is standing next to her husband, a handsome young man with a big smile on his lips and an arm around his girl.

The picture is passed around. The children want a look at their brother, their uncle, their father.

#

Joyce walks out of San Miguel. The iron fist of grief punches her in the gut. Her soul is marred by the senseless, meaningless loss of a husband, a father, a future. The pain in her belly spreads upward, gripping and wringing her heart, tearing at her throat, until she finally screams out to God in anger, cursing the dark bottomless sadness and hopelessness that blanket the community.

"Now you see what I see. Now you know what I know. Now you feel what I feel," whispers God.

"But is there hope?" Joyce asks through a waterfall of hot invisible tears.

Ministry

Chasing the memory of a joy swallowed by the vast emptiness of the past

I call out for its return only to receive the faint echo of my desire

My throat is hoarse and parched from longing

My body wrung of its strength to face the future that burdens me with its legions of unfulfilled dreams

I seek in the infinite depths of the chasm below my feet, straining my eyes to see what once was

Too deep and far gone, those moments that slipped by unnoticed, leave only a whiff of their presence

I step into the void and surrender all being into the hands of an eternal existence

Tuesday Morning Prayer

THE MORNING AIR is crisp and cool, adding freshness to the green hills under the blue skies—another beautiful morning. However, for Joyce and Amelia, there is no time to stop and take in this morning as they hurry up the hill. They are late for Tuesday prayer. They pick their way around the half-torn plastic bags of garbage that last night's storm flushed out of the overflowing trash bin onto the broken asphalt of the road. They throw their contribution into the now half-empty rusted bin.

Several children play in the tiny, fenced-in playground built by a community patron and hardware store owner a couple years back. They are from the *ranchitos* of the Invasion, a germ of a *barrio* that popped up overnight on the other side of the trash bin. The children spin around on the merry-go-around and swing upside-down on the monkey bars like little monkeys themselves. The oldest child calls out to Joyce and Amelia as they make their way up the hill, proud to claim acquaintance with these foreigners.

"¡Hola, Amelia! ¡Hola, Chinita!"

"*¡Hola, bella!*" Amelia and Joyce greet back.

"Do you know how truly beautiful and precious you are?" They silently ask the children.

Still climbing with the children watching on, Amelia and Joyce turn right at the first of three turns up the hill to the office.

Amelia and Joyce hurry on past the second and third turns, past the graveyard of trucks and buses that line the no-man's land where the ground is too unstable for even the most desperate to put up a *ranchito*, past the young men sitting outside their doorways with their vacant faces and their girlfriends half-asleep on their laps. They finally pass another trash bin that mark the entrance of Las Colinas.

The girls join Thomas and Agnes around a small wooden coffee table covered by a purple cloth. A lit candle in the middle of the table flickers, welcoming their presence. Thomas strums the guitar and opens Tuesday Prayer with a song that captures the crux of their ministry.

"He has shown you…"

Agnes joins in with her soprano. The girls follow along.

"Oh people!

What is good and what the Lord requires of us.

To do justice,

To love mercy,

And to walk humbly with the Lord."

After the song ends, Amelia stands up and leads the Tuesday ritual by saying the opening prayer. The rest of the team follows.

"Lord, open our lips," Amelia chants, calling the team to worship.

"and our mouth will sing your praise," the rest of the team responds.

Then the team prays.

They pray for each other.

They pray for Thomas's sore throat and Amelia's stomach problems, that the ailments not be anything too serious.

They pray for Joyce and her friendship with her host family.

They pray for Mario and his wife, that their neighbors are nicer to them and do not cut off their water any longer.

They pray for Evangelin and Enrique, for Evangelin's work and school.

They pray for Yolanda's recovery and for her to experience the gentle love of God in her pain.

They pray for Sr. Carlos and his remaining son, that they will know of grace and forgiveness.

They pray for the neighborhood, for safety from physical violence and landslides.

They pray for Sara and Adan, for financial provision and little Daniel's cough.

They pray for Gladys and her extended family to continue having tender hearts toward them and God.

They pray:

Our Father, who is in Heaven,

Holy be your name.

Your kingdom come, Your will be done, on Earth as it is in Heaven.

Give us this day, our daily bread,

And forgive us for our trespasses as we forgive those who trespass against us.

Lead us not into sin, but deliver us from evil.

At the end of the prayer, Agnes volunteers to do communion, to pray over the grape juice held in a clay chalice and the *campesino* bread on a wooden plate. The cup and the bread are passed around from one team member to the next.

"This is the blood shed for you, for the forgiveness of sins... This is the body broken for you..." they say to each other.

They hold the bread soaked with grape juice in their mouths, tasting the sourness of the bread and the sweetness of the juice, absorbing the presence of God into their beings, into their souls.

A Day of Rest

JOYCE AND AMELIA have waited eagerly for Wednesday. To have a complete day free to roam the city, to be inconspicuous, as much as a *gringa* and a *chinita* can be in the streets of Caracas—is a treat. Today, they will attempt to make their way to Sambil, the largest mall on the continent, five floors of consumerism at its finest. The girls take a jeep from Calle Diecinueve to their metro station, Ruiz Pineda. They catch a train to El Silencio, the transfer station in the middle of the city. They walk the mile-long *transferencia* underground tunnel to Capitolio in order to catch another train to Chacao, the metro station by the mall.

Chacao is on the east side of town, where the informal *camionetas* and jeeps do not run because the residents on that side of the town own cars. For a few hours that day, Joyce and Amelia will escape the *barrios* and enter into the world of car owners.

The *transferencia* is the bane of their Wednesday escapes. More than once the girls have chosen a destination that does not involve the *transferencia*. Instead, they caught a bus to Zoologico, the city zoo that provides a small oasis of peace on their side of the city when the majority of people are at work or at school.

But the girls find the extra bit of distance away from their *barrio* necessary once in a while to avoid burnout. To achieve that distance, both Joyce and Amelia have resigned themselves to the unavoidable commute. If they are really feeling ambitious and can get up early enough, they might even attempt the three-hour journey to the quaint Caracas suburb of

El Hatillo with its colorful colonial town square surrounded by chic chocolate shops and cafes. El Hatillo is the ultimate escape from the day-to-day reality of the *barrios*. It is a place where they can blend in with the other tourists buying souvenirs.

But today, they head to Sambil. By the time they arrive, it is already noon. Shoppers pour into the mall, scratching the newly waxed floors with their stiletto heels. Glass windows display the latest fashions of the hottest boutiques from around the world.

They head to the food court on the third floor to buy lunch. Joyce goes straight to Bonsai Sushi. She especially likes a sushi roll that comes with what she and Amelia have dubbed "the Venezuelan miracle sauce," which is a pink mixture made from ketchup and mayonnaise. They have found this sauce slathered on everything from crackers to potato chips. Amelia heads for all-American Mickey D's. They manage to find an empty table and sit down with their lunches.

"So what are you looking for again?" Joyce asks Amelia.

"A white top to go with the flower skirt my aunt sent me for a wedding. Something flattering but not too revealing..."

Most of what Amelia and Joyce wear on a day-to-day basis mimics the elastic glittery tanks and hip hugging jeans the girls and women wear in the *barrios*. "When in Rome, wear what the Romans wear," is one of the rules in the mission team's unwritten handbook. The looser, more muted articles of clothing they brought to Venezuela from the States are still packed away in their suitcases.

After searching for weeks in the streets and only finding flimsily-made tops that clung too tightly, Amelia's preference for quality has finally won out over her desire to fit in. She has decided that on special occasions, she will exercise her *gringa* privilege and take out her Visa card to swipe for something that might last beyond one wash.

"Let's go to Zara and Bershka and see what they have," Amelia suggests.

Zara and Bershka are two of Amelia's favorite stores in Caracas. At Zara, she once splurged on a pair of tight-fitting jeans that actually looked normal on her without cutting off her circulation.

Joyce and Amelia step into the world of silks and 100% cottons, clean lines and abstract prints. They brush elbows with the Venezuelan rich who pick through the neatly folded stacks of jeans and the racks of jackets and tops.

"What do you think of this shirt?" Amelia models for Joyce outside a spacious, well-lit Zara dressing room.

"Looks good, how much is it?"

"It's on sale, Bs. 60,000," Amelia answers with a hint of guilt, not sure if she can justify spending $30 on a shirt.

After scouring the entire store for a better deal but finding none, Amelia finally takes the shirt to the cash register. A tall, light-skinned, pimply teen scans the purchase and processes the payment.

With the errand completed, the girls spend what is left of the afternoon drifting from store to store, feeling the fine fabrics and trying on articles of clothing, allowing themselves to be tempted.

As the afternoon turns into night, the mall is even more packed, filled with teens strutting around as if they are stars from a *telenovela*. They are noticeably taller and fitter than those in the *barrios*, and most can ramble off a few sentences in English. Few stare and even fewer stop to say hi or practice their English with Joyce and Amelia. They can do that with their relatives in the States. The once-overs from men so common in the *barrios* are rarer here, and when given, are more discreet.

By the end of the day, rejuvenated, both girls are ready to leave the commercial gluttony of Sambil and return to their reality, nestled in the shimmering sea of twinkling lights of the *barrio* hills.

After tracing their steps back through the *transferencia*, after waiting in the long jeep line at the bottom of the hill, after a bumpy jeep ride, the girls unlock their apartment door with just a hint of the eastside lingering in their steps and minds. They are glad to be back in the *barrios* where kids scream out greetings as they run past on their way to buy *chucharias* at the *abasto*, where neighbors lounge in the streets, trading gossip and tapping their feet to the rhythm of raggaeton.

For the girls, tomorrow begins another week of living among the poor, another week of immersing themselves in the joys and the struggles, the boredom and chaos of *barrio* life.

Part II

JANE ZHANG

Thursday Nights

A MOONLESS NIGHT falls over San Juanito. Stars just out of reach twinkle brightly overhead. It is Thursday evening. The weekend has begun for Javier. He works another dab of gel into his already slicked-back jet-black hair and smiles at his reflection. A handsome young man smiles back.

"Javier!" he hears his friend Pablo call outside his window. "*¡Dale chamo!* Hurry it up! We don't have all night!"

"*¡Ya va! ¡Ya va!* I'm coming!" Javier pats down the last of the stubborn stray hairs behind his ears and steals a few more glances at himself. His attractiveness is something he has recently discovered, something he is learning to wield. With one last look in the mirror, Javier heads out the door.

Pablo is waiting outside with a couple of other young men. "*¿Listo?* Ready to party?" they greet him.

"*¡Por supuesto!*" Javier replies, trying out the sly smile he has been practicing in front of the mirror. The boys walk down the alley to their usual corner outside Sara and Adan's house and sit down next to their girlfriends. Juliana stands up, tugs her mini-skirt down over her long brown legs and sits down on Javier's lap, claiming him for the night. Javier shifts around until he finds a more comfortable position to accommodate Juliana's weight, weight that he enjoys having on his lap. It grounds him to the present, to the deepening darkness, to the laughter of his friends, to the sweet fragrance he could just barely detect as he nuzzles his face into the nape of Juliana's neck.

Pablo switches on the stereo he has brought and turns up the volume. Daddy Yankee blares out of the speakers. "*Ella le gusta la gasolina.* She likes gasoline," the boys sing, swaying the girls on their laps. *"Dame más gasolina.* Give me more gasoline," the girls reply, grinding their hips responsively.

Someone else pulls out a liter of boxed sangria and passes it around, ushering in the night.

The minutes and hours pass. The caresses become more daring, the jokes more crass, past exploits are brought out and paraded around. More members of the gang have joined the group. Javier holds Juliana closer to him, owning her, enjoying her warmth. *This is the life! This is the life! A girl on my lap, liquor in my belly and friends around me!* He thinks to himself. *If only nights like these could last forever.*

"Javier!" Pablo calls, jolting Javier out of his reverie. "Remember that time when we went over to Miguel's and we totally put that shit-face in his place? That was awesome! Remember how scared he was when you pulled out the pistol? Ha! Ha! He shit in his pants!"

"Man, that shit-face is such a mama's boy! We put him in his place, all right!" Javier replies. He reaches back into his memory and finds that night only a month ago when he carried a pistol for the first time. He was awakened in the night by Pablo, told to get dressed and meet up with their *panas* waiting outside. He had known the night was coming when he needed to prove his worth. As much as he had looked forward to that night, he was scared. *Did he have the* cojones *to pull it off?* He remembers thinking.

That night, Pablo had shoved the pistol into his hands. The metal felt heavier than he had anticipated. He remembers liking the feel of the sleek metal, cool in his hand, and the shivers of power running up his spine. He stood taller and walked with more confidence than he ever had before.

They had made their way across the valley, drinking in the night air and pounding down cheap liquor to strengthen their resolve.

The weekend prior, a gang of *malandros* had robbed Juan's uncle's *abasto* and given him a pretty bad beating. That night, they were out to get revenge. Their target was Miguel, the leader of that gang. Juan's cousin had staked out Miguel's house and said that there was a party there that night, a birthday party for Miguel's two-year-old niece. None of Miguel's gang was there. His mom would not allow them past the gate. By the time Pablo woke Javier up, the party was winding down—the perfect time to go over and make their statement.

When they arrived at Miguel's, reggaeton blasted from the lit living room. Only a few people still grinded away on the dance floor covered with confetti and candy wrappers.

The front gate was open.

How stupid and arrogant Miguel was! This was an invitation! Javier remembers thinking.

What happened afterward seemed like a dream, the best trip he had ever had.

Pablo led his *panas* into the house and grabbed Miguel by the collar from the back and yanked him away from the *puta* he was feeling up on the dance floor.

"You little shit!" Pablo yelled into Miguel's ear as he planted a fist into Miguel's kidney, doubling him over as Javier lent his right foot to Miguel's face.

"Next time you get it in your head that you want to come around and mess with my *panas*, remember this!" Javier added.

Perhaps it was the adrenaline that was pumping through his veins, perhaps it was the scared look in Miguel's eyes, perhaps it was the full and uninterrupted attention from the captive audience peering behind half-closed doorways and drawn curtains. Javier took out the pistol from his belt and pulled the trigger—at point blank. He wasn't so stupid as to kill the son-of-a-bitch; he had aimed at his knee. The explosion of the gun and Miguel's scream were simultaneous, piercing through the cold night air. They got themselves out of there pretty fast after that and celebrated afterward at Pablo's house. Hours later, when the excitement had worn off, he felt a twinge of guilt, but the alcohol had long dimmed his senses.

"Remember how scared he was, and how he cried?" Javier says, laughing. *I am the shit!* He revels to himself and grabs the sweet softness of Juliana's round bottom, trying to squeeze away the fear that has plagued him doggedly since the night he put the bullet in Miguel's knee. He tries not to think of the retaliation that looms in his dark future.

I am untouchable, I am the man! Javier chants to himself.

The Visitor

THE CAT PERCHES quietly on the tin corrugated metal that is Sara and Adan's roof. She looks up and down the *callejon*, her turf. Her power has become stronger and stronger over the last few decades as more and more *brujas* and *santeros* have joined her legion of slaves. Even the thin red string tied around babies' wrists for protection against the evil eye reinforces her dominance. Her subjects fear her wrath and would do anything to appease her.

Yet, recently, unnoticeable at first, a flicker of light has begun penetrating the web of darkness she has woven over the *barrio*. She has come to investigate and stamp out this ray of hope. The source of this light radiates up from the room below, glowing turquoise with an aura of freedom and emanating a whiff of sweet jasmine, repugnant to her senses. She peers through a rusted hole in the tin metal down at the people talking and laughing, ignoring her presence.

Sara has always been resistant to her influence. Although she has snuffed joy out of Sara's life numerous times, she can never manage to completely darken her life. The seed of hope is rooted too deep, lying dormant for even Sara, herself, to discern at times. The obstacles she places in Sara's life only periodically dent her spirit.

She thought that she had won Sara over by turning her parents against her. Not a day went by without Sara's stepmother physically and verbally abusing her, while her father, a cowering submissive, did nothing to intervene. But Adan's presence during that time revived her shriveled soul and brought her back to life. Their courtship evolved rapidly, and with a marriage proposal, Adan took Sara out of the toxic environment.

Her various attempts to insert a wedge between Sara and Adan have failed over and over again. The devotion the two have for each other somehow manages to mend what other couples could not let go of and forgive. Now, these pale-skinned visitors are blocking her efforts to get at Sara through her kids. These visitors have helped knit this family closer and closer together. They bring with them new spirits that attach themselves to the family like a fine coating of fairy dust, repelling the darkness she has worked so hard to cast over them.

One of these visitors has stayed the night—the first time this has happened. This catches her by surprise. No one who does not have relatives in this *barrio* ever stays the night because of the reputation of the violence and fear she has generated.

Her tail flicks once with displeasure before she rises and leaps over to another tin roof.

#

Joyce finishes arranging her supply of clothes, toiletries and books on a tiny bookshelf for her three-week stay with Sara and Adan. She sinks down into her makeshift foam mattress, folds her hands across her lap and looks about the damp, clutter-filled storage room that is to be her temporary home. She has waited months for this experience, to immerse herself completely—to live, minister, and be ministered to, here in San Juanito, one of the most dangerous and poverty-stricken neighborhoods this side of Caracas. She wants to claim some ministry as her own, to contribute in some way that will affirm the time she spends as a missionary with Little Steps in Venezuela. Whether anything significant will happen or not, she can at least say that she helped strengthen the team's ties to Sara's family and to this community.

For herself, she also looks forward to deepening her friendship with Sara. Ever since Joyce showed up one day at Sara's cleaning job, picked up the extra broom leaning against the wall and swept beside her, some of the formality Sara showed to the team melted away. That was almost a year ago, when Joyce spoke hardly any Spanish. Since then, Joyce has felt that Sara views her as a companion. Even though her Spanish has improved, they continue to communicate more through action than through words.

The *callejon* is now quiet with the noises of the night: the static humming of the naked light bulbs strung above the broken *callejon* steps, the gurgling of the water pipes, and the occasional footsteps and whispers carrying the last of the neighbors up to their homes after a long commute from the other side of town. Joyce changes into her nightgown. She pulls the cord strung to the lightbulb dangling from the ceiling and feels her way to the cot.

For a while, she lies there trying to fall asleep, trying to stop her racing imagination of what life will be like over the next three weeks. As the *barrio* grows quieter, her inner thoughts grow louder.

Just when her mind starts wandering into the realm of semi-conscious dreams, loud bangs jolt her awake.

"*¿Yoli? ¿Yoli?*" Joyce hears Sara's voice whispering outside the door.

"*¿Si?*" Joyce replies from under the covers.

"*¿Estás bien?*" Sara asks, "*No te preocupes. Son los malandros.* These thugs have been more actively lately. We are safe inside. Don't worry. Try to sleep…*"

"*¡Bueno, gracias!*" Joyce answers as the fear and excitement churn inside her. She feels a sense of confirmation that she is no longer in the protective safety of either her team or her neighbors in her own *barrio*.

The shots and shouts of the *malandros* outside slowly quiet, but she can no longer sleep. Joyce hears the cautious steps of a cat prowling on the corrugated roof above her. She hears the scratching of cockroaches on the plywood walls. She hears the faint drips of a leaky water pipe at the other end of the house.

The foreignness of her surroundings and the adrenaline pumping through her keep her alert no matter how much she wants sleep to overtake her mind and to stop the storytellers from weaving nightmares.

God, she prays silently, Replace my thoughts.

From the recesses of her mind, a verse she read that day surfaces.

You will not fear the terror of the night,
Nor the arrow that flies by day,
Nor the pestilence that stalks the darkness
Nor the destruction that wastes at noonday.

I will not fear the terror of the night nor the pestilence that stalks the darkness, Joyce chants to herself.

In her mind's eye, she sees an orb of light surrounding her, expanding brighter and brighter, driving out the hidden darkness from the corners of the room, driving away the crawling critters of the night. The light envelopes her like a warm blanket, cocooning her in its warmth.

I will not fear the terror of the night nor the pestilence that stalks the darkness, she repeats over and over until she slips into a dreamless sleep.

Above her, perched under the cool glow of the moonlight, the cat hisses.

Full Immersion

The food you eat, I eat
The steps you take, I follow

When the rooster crows, I wake with you
When the sun sets, I rest by your side

This is my promise, this is my call
I vow to be present
Here
Heart, mind and soul

Your worries, I share
Your laughter, I echo

Burdens, I will help you carry
Trials, I will help you bear

This is my promise, this is my call
I vow to be present
Here
Heart, mind and soul

Sara's Story

"I HAVE 22 *hermanos*," Sara begins.

"22 brothers and sisters?" Joyce asks, not believing her ears. She is sitting at the kitchen table, watching Sara stand over the kitchen sink disemboweling the night's dinner.

"Yes, 22 *hermanos*: one brother, one sister and 20 half-brothers and sisters. My two siblings and I are from my dad's first marriage to Mariana. When they separated, my dad brought the three of us here to San Juanito. He remarried my stepmom, Stefania. She gave him ten kids. You know her, too. She lives at the top of the hill with Sofia who comes by here all the time. Sofia runs around with some of the younger kids. But she's a good girl, doesn't get into too much trouble as long as she stays away from all the guys who hound her. She doesn't know any better, though." Sara taps her head, referring to Sofia's lack of sense when it comes to boys.

"My mom also remarried and had ten kids with her new husband. That's 22 not including me," Sara explains. She settles herself down next to Joyce by the kitchen table and smiles at her guest, whose eyes shine with amazement. "My mom's ten kids stay with her in Los Telares. They sometimes visit. It's one huge party. My *hermanos* and half-*hermanos* on my dad's side, they are all here in San Juanito. Most of them live up the *callejon*. You know Jorge and Edna, they are my full *hermanos*. I'm closest with them. You've also met Ronald and Luz, they still live with my stepmom. And I'm sure you also recognize the others, at least by sight. Pedro, he's the one that is always down by the Redoma, collecting cans and such. He lives in the streets and never seems to be able to settle down permanently anywhere."

With each description, Sara paints her family tree with its numerous branches shooting every which way. Brothers, sisters, aunts and uncles, cousins twice or thrice removed, marriages and breakups tying her to the majority of the residents that enclose her from above and below.

"So where are you in the line-up?" Joyce asks.

"I'm the oldest," Sara answers.

"What was it like growing up with such a big family? Did you have a lot of responsibilities?"

"I did everything."

"What is everything?"

"The cooking, the cleaning, taking care of the kids. My dad was sick and Stefania was always pregnant, ordering me around from her bed, swatting me with a stick when I got too close to her. My *hermano*, Jorge, helped me some when he got old enough. We would carry buckets of water up and down the *callejon* steps for a few *bolívares*. Back then, we didn't have pipes to bring water up the hill. It took ten trips to fill a tank, and we would make maybe Bs. 5. *Bolívares* were worth a lot more back then. For Bs. 10, you could buy at least a bag of rice.

"Stefania didn't care much for Jorge, Edna and me. She treated us terrible. My dad didn't ever intervene. He didn't seem to see any of it. When I got older, about Franyeli's age, Stefania wouldn't let me out of the house unless it was to work. She'd call me a *puta* and my dad believed her. My life was so miserable."

Memories of those hard years etch themselves across Sara's brow. She pauses and looks out the kitchen door into the past.

When she continues again, a smile has swept away the dark lines. "Then I met Adan. He had just moved here with Monica, his daughter from a previous marriage. Did you know Adan is from the West, from a little town bordering Colombia? Anyway, he brought Monica all the way from the *frontera*. They rented a room across the *callejon* from us. He would come by and hand me sweets through the window after work. One day, he asked me if I'd like to go out with him. Of course I said yes, but only if my dad said it was ok.

"The next day, Adan knocked on our door. Stefania opened the door and asked Adan what he wanted. He said he wanted to take me out. My stepmom said no. 'What do you want from that *puta*?' She asked Adan. My dad was sitting right there by the front door, but he said nothing.

"Later, when I asked my dad why he didn't say anything, he said he believed what my stepmom said, that I was a slut." As Sara says the last few words, her face darkens with pain at the memory.

Sara takes a deep breath and continues, "Lucky for me, Adan was not fazed by my stepmom, and my dad thought Adan was a nice guy and allowed me to go out with him. I was really happy! But on the day Adan was supposed to take me out, Stefania said I could only go out after I finished cleaning the house and doing all the laundry. I didn't want to argue, so I did what I was told. After I had finished everything, my stepmom still said I couldn't go out. My dad just shrugged his shoulders.

"I finally had enough. '*Basta!*' I told her, 'I am going to go with or without your permission.' She started calling me names and hitting me, throwing my clothes out the door. I was so angry I didn't care.

"Adan had come by at that time and took me away. We walked and walked without saying a word. And when I cried, he just held me. After that, I had nowhere to go, so I moved in with him and his daughter. About a month after I moved in with him, we went to the courthouse and got married. That night, we went to a hotel in the La India neighborhood, and he showed me the way of husband and wife," Sara smiles shyly.

"And after that?" Joyce asks, curious to know what happened after Prince Charming rescued Cinderella from the evil stepmother.

"After that? Well, we lived like a family. It was so nice! Adan really cared for me. He saved up some money and bought a little plot of land from a neighbor. At first, we could only afford to put up a *ranchito*. It was here, where we are sitting, right here where the kitchen is. Where the living room and the bedrooms are, we had a big yard with a few chickens. Over time, we were able to add more rooms, put down a concrete floor, build up the walls with cinder blocks. And here we are!" Sara finishes her story, holding her palms open as if showing Joyce the calluses the years of hard work had left.

"And the kids?" Joyce asks, wanting to hear more.

"The kids we didn't have till a couple years after we got married. Adan wanted us to get to know each other first before having kids. When David was born, he was so weak. We nursed him and took care of him the best we could, not knowing whether he was going to survive or not. Franyeli came out with a full head of hair, as strong as a boar! Perhaps that is why David is so close to me, and Franyeli to Adan. We didn't think we would have any more after Franyeli, but five years later, Daniel came. After that, I had my tubes tied. Three is enough. That's what I keep telling Edna, but she wants more. How is she going to take care of them?"

"But your sister only has two."

"Edna can barely handle those two. Her husband doesn't help out at all and she can't manage to keep a stable job." From there, Sara returns to her favorite subject, the *telenovela* lives of her twenty-two siblings.

Work

ADAN WAKES. Sara shifts next to him, subconsciously adjusting to his wakefulness. Daniel, their youngest, is sandwiched between them, sleeping fitfully as he struggles to breathe, wheezing with his asthmatic lungs. The morning light has not yet penetrated the crack between the metal window shutters. Adan sits up and swings his legs over the edge of the bed.

Today, there is work! Adan thinks to himself. He looks forward to the days when work waits for him, when he can wake with the knowledge that today he will provide for his family. That knowledge feeds him, feeds his soul. The days without any prospect of work drain him. Those days stretch endlessly, blending in with the stench of despair hanging over the *barrios*.

Today he will need to find a motor for Mrs. Doris's old washing machine. The motor finally gave out after innumerable fixes.

It shouldn't be too hard. People on the other side of town are upgrading from their older models, Adan thinks. I should get the part for this machine pretty easily.

He changes out of his pajamas and into his work clothes before going to the kitchen to heat up a couple of leftover *arepas* from the night before.

Sara follows him up the steps to the kitchen.

"*Buenos, mi amor,*" Adan greets his wife.

"*Buenos,*" Sara replies sleepily, taking the pan from Adan's hand. Adan walks to the little sink he has installed outside the kitchen door and washes away the night. Looking through the chain-linked fence in front of the sink, he can see that the lush *lechosa* tree on his neighbor's property has begun to bear fruit. The green pear-sized *lechosas* shine with the morning dew. Adan wishes he had more property to grow some fruit trees of his own. Stowing the wish away with the million others for the moment, he grabs the towel hanging on the fence, dries his face and turns back inside for breakfast.

By the time he walks back into the kitchen, Sara already has the two piping hot *arepas* reheated and stuffed with black beans and shredded *queso duro*. Adan stuffs one in his mouth and wraps up the other one for later, in case he does not get paid and cannot buy anything to eat.

Adan walks down the *callejon*. He turns right at the bottom of the hill and continues to the metro station. He waits on the platform with the other commuters and crowds into the train car when it finally pulls up, already jammed with people.

Skip down the steps.

Squeeze into a crowded train car.

Rush through the *transferencia*.

Wait for the transfer.

Push into another packed car.

Climb out of the metro.

Catch a bus.

Hop onto another.

After a good hour-and-a-half of commuting, Adan finally walks into his favorite *ferreateria* in Chacaito. Every inch of floor and wall space is covered by half-assembled appliances and their parts.

"Buenos, Tomas."

"*¡Buenos, Adan!* What are you looking for today?" The proprietor responds.

"A motor for a washing machine."

A few minutes later, the two men stand over the counter, examining the four or five motors the proprietor has brought out from the backroom.

"None of these came off of the model you mentioned yesterday over the phone. That model's too old. Maybe five or six years ago, someone on this side of town might have ungraded from that model, but not anytime recently. These are the closest I found," the proprietor explains.

"That's ok, I can probably adjust this one to fit," Adan holds up a greasy motor. "How much?"

"Bs. 40,000," Tomas throws out a number. He knows Adan is not a bargaining man, so he gives him a fair price.

"That sounds good. *Gracias,*" Adan says. He pulls out two Bs. 20,000 bills and hands them to the proprietor before picking up the motor.

"*A la orden,*" Tomas replies. "Anytime."

"*Bueno, bueno,*" Adan heads out of the store, happy with the smoothness of the transaction.

Back on the bus, the bus transfer, the metro, the *transferencia* and back to Ruiz Pineda.

He gets in line for the jeep to Sra. Doris's *barrio* across the valley from San Juanito. His stomach growls, reminding him that he has an *arepa* in his pocket. He takes it out and chews thoughtfully. He thinks through each step of replacing a washing machine's broken motor, including the various adjustments he will have to make for the motor to fit the older model.

By the time he makes it up to Sra. Doris's house, he has already worked out what he will need to do. He is familiar with Sra. Doris's machine, having made repairs to it at various occasions over the past years since Sra. Doris first hired him.

After over an hour on his knees, the machine is whirling beautifully for him. Sra. Doris hands Adan four 20,000 *bolívar* notes and thanks him.

"De nada," Adan replies thankfully.

Down at the Redoma again, Adan steps into the *panadería*.

We'll need a bit more food the next few weeks to feed Yoli, Adan thinks to himself as he picks up several loaves of bread and a kilo each of sliced ham and *queso duro*.

With the change jingling in his pocket, he walks up the *callejón*, stopping to greet and chat with neighbors along the way, taking his time to savor a successful day.

Competition

DAVID WAKES TO the rattling of Daniel's cough in the next room. The room is pitch black, the air damp. His sister Franyeli is fast asleep in the bunk below. Lying still, he feels his lungs expand and contract; he listens to his heart beating in his ears. Today is the swim competition. Eight laps, four different strokes. Rafael will be in the lane third from the left, right next to him. Rafael is a good friend. He lent David his extra Speedo last week for the competition.

Wearing old tattered knock-offs would have been embarrassing. David's face flushes at the thought.

Franyeli stirs and talks nonsensically in her sleep. *Probably dreaming of eating a whole* pan de jamón *all by herself.* David chuckles at the image.

He rolls toward the wall and reaches out to touch where the face of Belinda, his favorite pop star, should be on the wall. The poster crinkles to the touch.

I will be a big movie star someday. I will be discovered by a talent scout. Then I will bump into Belinda at a party in one of those clubs on the other side of town I have only heard about. We will catch each other's eyes across the room. She will separate herself from all the other hot guys surrounding her and walk toward me, working her way across the crowded dance floor in some slinky dress and big dangly earrings. I will be standing turned slightly toward her with a confident smile on my lips, waiting for her to come to me.

Yah, right! That would be Rafael. I will be the skinny guy next to Rafael, Rafael's sidekick. David finally shakes himself free of his fantasies.

Belinda's face slowly becomes visible, lit by the beams of morning light shining through the curtain. Eyes twinkling, she smiles seductively down at David.

#

In the afternoon, David is bent over the diving platform alongside his peers, poised to leap into the water. To his left is Rafael, his friend, his foe. Rafael's powerful frame arches with beauty and strength. Like most of his classmates, David is drawn to Rafael's charisma. He walks the hallways exuding the unconscious self-confidence of the privileged. His words hold more weight; his attention is more coveted. David's friendship with Rafael has elevated his own status among his peers. With a sheepish, self-conscious awareness, he knows that his own quiet charm is starting to merit its own attention, particularly in the last year or so as his body has begun to fill out his lanky 15-year-old frame. But standing near naked next to Rafael in the secondhand Speedo Rafael has lent him, David feels exposed, diminished in size and stature.

The gun explodes, rippling across the chlorinated pool, hushing the chatter of the audience for just a split second. David dives into the water after Rafael, who glides effortlessly through the air, breaking the calm surface of the pool. The race is a combination swim, one full length each of free style, breast, backstroke and finally the butterfly—David's weakest stroke.

David takes the lead at the first turn. His slender frame compensates for his lack of strength. But by the third turn, Rafael, with his powerful kicks, has caught up with him. At the fifth turn, the boys are swimming shoulder to shoulder, raising their arms over their heads, synchronized almost perfectly as they propel themselves through the water. At the sixth turn, the boys kick off the wall and explode out of the water. Their bodies arch and soar like eagles through the air with arms spread wide, enveloping their open futures before them.

Too soon, Rafael's powerful strokes and dolphin kicks push him far ahead of the rest of the pack. Out of the corner of his eye, David cannot help but feel both envy and admiration for Rafael's form and beauty.

Seconds later, Rafael pulls himself out of the pool with a broad smile on his lips and a sparkle in his eyes. Beads of water glisten on his tanned, sculpted Romanesque body. David, finishing second behind Rafael, holds onto the side of the pool to catch his breath. He squints against the glare reflecting off of Rafael's body and sees his friend's hand reaching down for him. He grabs Rafael's extended hand and pulls his thin frame out of the water. *Coming in second is nothing to be ashamed of, especially after a sure winner,* David reassures himself. *I have worked hard and done well.*

When all the meets finish, the boys line up next to each other in a row of swimmers waiting for the awards ceremony. Their principal, coach and an entourage of important people whom David does not recognize walk before the swimmers and present each with a medal.

With his dangling from his neck, David scans the audience seated on the other side of the chain-linked fence surrounding the pool. His mom, siblings and Joyce are sitting in the front row cheering him on. He smiles, grateful to have their presence and support. He knows that in their eyes, he is the one they have come to watch, the one who matters.

In the small San Juanito pond David swims in, he is a big fish.

Bible Study

ONCE AGAIN, THOMAS and Joyce, Sara and Adan sit in a circle in Sara and Adan's living room. Thomas and Joyce are on the couch next to piles of unfolded clothes; Sara and Adan are in a chair and on a stool across from them. Their three children, leaning on one another, sit on the steps leading up to the kitchen.

Once again, the rain beats down on the tin roof, a soothing gentle roar in the background. The air is saturated with a peaceful joy.

This ritual of the weekly visit is an anchor. For Sara and Adan, these visits are their Sabbaths, a time to rest, a time to unload, a time to share their burdens with people whom they have come to consider family. This is the best type of family, the type that does not dump their heavy loads of worry on them but takes on theirs instead. For Thomas and Joyce, these times represent a dogged faithfulness to the work of God in San Juanito, of possible moments to witness God's love and truth penetrating the darkness of the *barrios*.

After the guests settle in, Sara gets up to go make the *cafecitos*.

"I'll do it," Joyce volunteers. After two weeks of living with Sara and Adan, Joyce has subconsciously slipped into the rhythms of the family, taking up her share of work in a playing house kind of way.

Sara, without a second thought, sits back down in her chair and continues updating Thomas on the week's developments in San Juanito. "Jaime, El Lobo, is finally feeling better. You know that I am working for him, don't you? I've been going over there to cook and clean for him ever since he was shot."

To give her guests a colorful picture of Jaime, Sara adds, "He is the *lobo* with all that body hair he puts on display, always walking around without a shirt on. He also verbally assaults every woman and girl with sexual innuendos. I just have to snap back at him once in a while." Sara looks over at Adan to see if her comment has drawn out a jealous reaction from her husband. It has not. She smiles, secure in the trust she shares with the only man she has ever known.

"Aren't you related to him?" Thomas asks, never quite sure who is or is not related to Sara.

"Yes, he's my uncle. But he's like that with everyone. He has been especially keen on Yolí," Sara chuckles. "Isn't that right, Yolí?" she jokes just as Joyce enters the room with a tray of *cafecitos* and bread.

Joyce smiles a half smile, playing along.

"*Sí,*" she says and rolls her eyes at Sara, pretending to consort with her on an inside joke. She succeeds by drawing a laugh from Sara.

Thomas looks at Joyce with concern and awe. He is concerned that in the two weeks Joyce has been living in San Juanito she has been under too much stress, and he is in awe of how well she seems to be holding up.

When the *cafecito* cups are emptied and the bread eaten, Thomas turns the conversation to the Bible. He is eager not to miss another opportunity to move forward with the series of ten Bible stories that highlight the main concepts of the Christian faith. Their hope in developing this series is that the stories will give the families they work with some grounding from which their faith can grow.

In the past two months since they started the series, they have only covered a few of the stories because of the unpredictability of Sara and Adan's lives. The other weeks have been consumed with various crises involving one or another of the extended relatives in Sara's clan.

This week's story is about Moses. Thomas unrolls a poster on which the team has illustrated the stories in simple imagery, threading them together to form one clear message of God's justice and grace.

Adan leans forward, looking at the strangely familiar pictures. There is the garden, the rainbow, the tablets of the Ten Commandments, the cross, the lamb, the throne of God. They are all there, images he associates with Christianity.

Thomas walks his audience through the first three pictures, recalling the discussions they have had the weeks before about Adam and Eve, about Noah, about Abraham. "This week, we are going to look at the story of Moses. What do you know about Moses?"

"Yes, Moses, I know him," Adan says with a smile of confidence. "He was the man that brought the people of Israel out of Egypt; he turned his staff into a snake before the Pharaoh; he divided the Red Sea; he brought the Ten Commandments down from Mt. Sinai." He points at the cartoon tablets in the drawing.

"We saw his story on TV," Sara pipes in. When she sees the puzzled looks on her guests' faces, she adds, "Every year during *Semana Santa*, the TV stations show all the Bible movies. There is one about Abraham, and another about Jesus. We have learned all about the stories in the Bible from these movies!"

They listen to Sara as she recounts the highlights of the movies. Thomas appreciates Sara's energy, her desire to engage.

"That's great!" he says. He smiles and pauses to acknowledge Sara's contribution to the conversation before redirecting the conversation to scripture. "Well, we are going to look closely at what is written in the Bible about Moses. Do you have your Bible?"

"Sí, Eva gave me hers before she left," Sara pulls out the Spanish Bible Eva had given her as a farewell present before she was swept away by her fiancé back to the States. Sara holds the gift with the same gentle care she takes with the other memories she has of Eva.

Eva in San Miguel, Eva in Calle Diecinueve, Eva in San Juanito, Thomas thinks and is humbled by what a lasting impact Eva's ministry had. He is constantly reminded of Eva's enduring imprint and thankful for the foundations of friendship she laid with the families they continue to work with.

"Let's turn to Exodus 3," Thomas says.

After finding her place in her bilingual Bible, Joyce leans over to Sara and helps her locate the passage.

When it appears that everyone has located it, Thomas asks, "Can someone read?"

Sara looks up eagerly, and with a nod from Adan, she begins to read, enunciating each word carefully, "Now Moses was tending the flock of Jethro his father-in-law, the priest of Midian, and he led the flock to the far side of the desert and came to Horeb, the mountain of God."

Sara pauses. The pronunciations of foreign names of people and places tire her. She looks over at Adan and hands him the Bible. "You finish reading it," she requests of her husband.

"You are doing a good job," Adan assures his wife before taking the Bible from her outstretched hands. After finding where Sara left off, he continues reading, "There the angel of the Lord appeared to him in flames of fire from within a bush. Moses saw that though the bush was on fire it did not burn up. So Moses thought, 'I will go over and see this strange sight—why the bush does not burn up.' When the Lord saw that he had gone over to look, God called to him from within the bush, 'Moses! Moses!' And Moses said, 'Here I am.'"

When Adan finishes, the group falls silent, looking to Thomas to lead the conversation.

Thomas turns around and faces Adan and Sara's three children sitting behind them. "Let's read the passage again," he says. "David, will you read the passage again for us?" Thomas smiles an invitation for the whole family to join the conversation.

David returns the smile. "*Bueno*," he answers.

With more formal classroom education than both of his parents combined, he mumbles flawlessly through the passage as fast as he can.

After David finishes, Thomas holds the silence for a long second before he asks, "We know that God chose Moses to lead the Israelites out of Egypt. My question for you is this: Why did God choose Moses? What character traits did Moses possess that qualified him to be chosen?"

Like most questions Thomas asks, Joyce knows the answer is simple, yet not always apparent. She smiles. She loves watching Thomas lead studies like this one. She sees in him an innate ability to tune in to the Spirit and allow the conversation to meander without fear of where it is going.

"I don't see anything special about Moses," Sara answers innocently, looking up at Thomas to see if she has missed anything.

Thomas nods. He looks around the room to see if anyone else has a different answer.

"Adan?" Thomas asks when no one else speaks. "How about you? What do you think?"

"Well, I don't see anything either, but God must have chosen him because of some special characteristic he had," Adan answers, giving his best guess.

"And what were those characteristics?" Thomas pushes.

Adan scans the words lying before him in black and white. His brow furrows deeper and deeper as he tries to find an answer.

After a moment, Joyce senses Adan's frustration. Wanting to help the conversation along, she adds, "I don't think there was anything special about Moses. He was a rash man. If we read what he did before, we learn that he ran away from Egypt, we see that he impulsively killed a man out of anger. And if we read what he did after God called him to go ask the Pharaoh to let the Israelites leave, we learn that Moses was not confident in himself because he told God that he was not the right person for the job."

Sara is happy Joyce has confirmed her initial response but is concerned that she is not on the same page with Adan, who has not yet abandoned searching the passage for a characteristic that warrants God's favor on Moses.

"But Moses must have been a righteous man, or had some characteristic that made him a good leader," Adan says. In his mind, he sees Charlton Heston's imposing figure with the flowing white beard standing on Mount Sinai. "There must be something."

"Well, what does the Bible say?" Thomas asks.

Minutes pass, Adan reads and rereads the passage. He searches for something in the Bible to confirm his conviction that Moses merited selection. He tries desperately to reconcile the image of Charlton Heston with the words in front of him.

"*Nada*," Adan finally says as he lays down the Bible on his lap and looks up in amazement. "Moses had no special attributes that made him a better candidate to lead the Israelites out of Egypt."

Again, Thomas holds the silence, allowing this discovery to set in.

"So Moses was just an average guy?" Thomas asks to confirm.

Everyone around the dimly lit room tentatively nods.

"Then why did God choose Moses?" Thomas asks the next logical question.

Again, a silence. Again Adan picks up the Bible, trying to absorb the meaning.

"Because he is God," Adan finally says with conviction. In his mind, a new flame flickers and catches. *God chooses us not because we merit it, but because he is God!*

Joyce smiles. Once again, she recognizes the work of the Spirit in the *barrios* and is humbled again by how God speaks when given the space. She looks over at Thomas and sees her smile reflected in his face.

Beach Day

ADAN DOES NOT have enough money. He does not want to take the money Joyce has offered. He wants to pay for the beach trip Joyce and Sara have planned for the family. He wants to provide for his family and guest. But he does not have enough money. The trip will not happen.

"But Adan! This is a token of thanks for your hospitality! You and Sara are like my *tios*, and David, Franyeli, Daniel, my *primos*," Joyce says, pressing the bills into Adan's hand.

"No, no. We can't go to the beach anyway. I might have to work tomorrow," Adan refuses.

"But Adan, we've been planning to go to the beach for a week now. The kids said they haven't gone in years. And, well, I really want to go with your family!" Joyce continues to argue.

"Well," Adan says, "perhaps you can go with Sara and the kids."

Sara and the kids in the next room smile at each other, happy that Adan has finally relented.

#

The house is fully awake. They will need an early start if they want to get to the beach before noon. It is Saturday. The metro and buses will be packed with shoppers and beachgoers. If they leave early enough, they will hopefully be able to find seats. Adan is in the kitchen, frying up a few *arepas* for the family to eat before their trip.

"Are you sure you can't go?" Joyce asks again, hoping Adan has changed his mind overnight.

"No, I need to wait to see if I get any work today," Adan answers, smiling at Joyce's pushiness. "Perhaps I can join you guys later if I am free. Which beach are you going to?"

"Playa Camuri Chico. You can catch a bus to the beach at La Hoyada metro station," Joyce says, doubting that Adan will show, but still hoping he will. *It would be great if the family had a day out together,* Joyce thinks, *memories to live on when times get tough in the future.*

"Ok, I'll text you guys later and let you know if I can make it or not."

"*¡Vamos, Yoli!*" David calls from the living room. He is looking forward to this trip, to get away from San Juanito, from the trash and grime that constantly remind him of how trapped he is. He cannot wait to leave. The only anchor he has to this place is his mom, his best friend. He is tired of seeing her tired all the time, stressed about money all the time. A trip to the beach will take her mind off of the relentless demands constantly banging on their door at all hours of the day and night.

"*¡Ya va!*" Joyce calls back to David before making one last appeal. "Adan, I really hope you can make it."

Sara joins them in the kitchen, giddy to be going to the beach. Adan puts his arms around his wife and kisses her. "So you are finally sneaking out to play, are you?" Adan jokes.

"About time!" Sara quips.

"Here's some money," Adan hands Sara Bs. 60,000, the last of the money he made during the last couple of weeks. He hopes Sra. Julia will call with work, he is depending on Sra. Julia to feed his family this week. "Don't spend it all on sweets."

"Of course not!" Sara replies, pretending to be insulted.

"Here, take the *arepas* and eat them on the way to the beach." Adan wraps the *arepas* in a paper towel and hands them to Sara. "You guys have fun," he says and pecks his wife on the cheek.

#

A BonIce man takes a break under the tall palm trees swaying under the weight of the noon heat.

"*¿¿Ceviche?!*" yells a bare-chested vendor wearing torn shorts, grinning at the scantily clad girls baking under the Caribbean sun.

Hours pass. Crystal blue waters crash against glistening wet bodies, sweeping away sand, days and nights of sickness, fear, worry.

Music rides the waves into the horizon, harmonizing to the rhythms of the sea.

Paradise.

Joyce lathers herself head to toe with sunscreen she brought from the States. Though she tans better than her white teammates, her skin is still not as genetically adapted as the Venezuelans are to the intensity of the equatorial sun.

Sara puts a couple of dabs on her face just to try it out. As for the children, they laugh good-humoredly before running into the ocean wave's embrace.

"*¡Mamá! ¡Yolí!* Join us!" David calls from the turquoise water before he and Franyeli swim farther into the bright ocean.

Daniel, left behind at the edge of the water, runs back to Sara and Yolí.

"*¡Ven, Mamá!* Come play with me!" Daniel begs. He flashes an ear-to-ear smile and tugs at Sara's arm.

"*¡Ya va!* We're coming." Sara relents, unable to resist the request of her youngest. She stands up and dusts the sand off of her body and holds her hand out to Joyce. "*Vamanos, Yolí, Vamanos a jugar.*"

Joyce grabs Sara's hand and hoists herself up. "*¡Sí, vamanos!*"

\#

Night has already fallen by the time Joyce and the family make it back to San Juanito. Their ascent is slow. Men and women stand outside their homes with their kids chirping around their feet, eating *cucharias* and running in circles. Since Sara knows everyone on her way uphill to her house, the small party stops every few steps to catch up on gossip and relay their adventure of the day.

"*¡Hola!*" people greet the party.

"Just come back from the beach?" they ask, feeling the residual warmth of the sun radiating off their faces.

Their party first stops in front of the *abasto* situated opportunistically above the elementary school at the bottom of the hill. The *abasto*'s frozen juice pops and candy sell well most days and nights.

"This is Yolí," Sara introduces Joyce with an air of diplomacy and pride. "She is staying with us for a few weeks."

"*¡A chinita!* Does she speak Spanish?" the proprietor asks Sara.

"*Sí,*" Joyce interjects, eager to take part in the conversation.

"*¡Que chévere!* You speak Spanish!" The proprietor turns to Joyce to greet her. "*¡Bienviendos!*"

"Are you *japonesa?*" he asks.

"No."

"*¿Koreana?*"

"No."

"*¿China?*"

"*Sí.*"

"*¿Es lo mismo, no?*" the proprietor asks rhetorically.

"No. The three actually have very distinct cultures developed independently over hundreds and thousands of years." Joyce answers.

"*¡Es lo mismo! ¡Como venezolanos y colombianos!*" the proprietor pushes.

"*Es similar.*" Not wanting to argue, Joyce relents to his efforts to connect on some commonality.

"Well, you are the first *china* to visit San Juanito! We've had *gringos*, but a *china!*" the proprietor says with pride.

"Gracias," Joyce answers, not knowing what else to say. She has discovered that in Venezuela, she is neither American nor Chinese American. She is, first and foremost, Chinese— marked by her almond eyes and admired for her straight black hair. As much as she benefits from her Chineseness (like not being asked if she is a part of the CIA as her white teammates are), she is, at times, tired of explaining that she does not work at the one Chinese restaurant in the Redoma or own an import store that sells all things plastic *hecho en china*. She does enjoy owning the fact that she is the cousin of Jackie Chan.

"You guys are good business people," the proprietor says. "But usually you guys don't venture into the *barrios*. There's not much money to be made up here. What are you doing up here?"

"I'm with the other *gringos* actually, with Piecitos De Dios. Do you know any of them?" Joyce describes the tall skinny gringo, the short-haired German gringa who sometimes brings her kids, her blond housemate, and Eva, who had passed for a Venezuelan with her dark hair and Venezuelan Spanish and mannerisms back when she still worked with Little Steps.

"Sí, *los conozco*. I've seen them before. What do you guys do?"

"We are *misioneros*. We work with different churches in this part of Caracas, including the Catholic Church in the Redoma. We are also involved in different programs in the *barrios* like the kids club here in San Juanito."

"And you are staying with Sara and Adan?"

"Sí. Sara and Adan have been really hospitable to our team." Joyce nods to Sara.

"And you know how to make *arroz chino*?" the proprietor returns to the path of questioning Joyce is very familiar with.

"Sí, I can make fried rice."

"I love *arroz chino*," the proprietor says, beaming fondly at the *barrio's* resident *chinita*. "Especially *arroz chino con los camerones*!"

"Next time I make *arroz chino*, I'll bring some by!" Joyce offers.

Having satisfied his curiosity, he turns his attention to Sara, asking after Adan and inquiring about the goings-on up the hill.

The conversation repeats predictably the rest of the hike up the hill.

"*¡Bienviendos!*"

"*¡Mi chinita! ¡Mi bella! ¡Mi corazon!*"

"*¡Hola mi amor!*"

"*¡Hagame arroz chino como lo hacen en las tiendas Chinas, mi chinita preciosa!*"

A trail of greetings and gossip follow the group up to their house.

"Why is a *chinita* staying with Sara and Adan?"

"What does she do?"

"Does she work?"

"At least she knows how to cook *arroz chino*."

Adan is waiting. "How was your day?" he kisses Sara affectionately on the lips.

"It was great!" Sara replies, still beaming from all the excitement of the day.

"And Yolí? Did you enjoy the beach?" Adan asks Joyce.

"*Sí*, Adan. But I wish you had been there with us. We had so much fun! And you? How was your day?"

"*Bien, Bien*," Adan says. He touches the bills in his pocket, glad that Sra. Julia had called after all. He has something to show for not going with his family to the beach. Providing for his family is his top priority. His family having some fun is the same as he himself having fun.

"So tell me, what did I miss?"

"Guess who we bumped into?" Sara asks excitedly.

"*¡Mi familia!*" Sara answers without pausing to give Adan a chance to guess. "They were all there from Los Telares. They had pooled their money together and rented a bus for a beach trip. We were able to get a ride home with them—only halfway though."

"They dropped us off at the side of the highway. You know, where the highway splits, right after the tunnel that connects Los Telares to the rest of Caracas," David pipes in. "We had to hitchhike back to Caracas!"

"You did what?!" Adan asks in shock.

"This guy in a SUV stopped and gave us a ride. He turned out to be a Christian. What a blessing! I didn't know what we were going to do if he hadn't come along," Sara's explanation rolls off of her tongue. "He dropped us off at the La Paz metro station. Then we caught the metro back to Ruiz Pineda."

"Well, it's good that you guys made it back in one piece," Adan says in amazement. "So how was the beach?"

"It was great!" David answers with laughter in his eyes. "We got there early and had half the beach to ourselves before everyone else showed up. You should have seen mom getting thrown around by the waves!"

Adan looks at Sara, who is grinning ear-to-ear. "The waves kept knocking me over. I'm all bruised!" Sara says.

Adan reaches out and pulls his wife to him, "Well, you are safe now." *Safe from the waves, strangers and unpredictable calamities,* Adan thinks to himself.

#

Up in the kitchen, the kids and Joyce are still joking around. "Tell Franyeli to say it," David urges Joyce.

"Say what?" Joyce feigns ignorance. "What we taught Franyeli to say this morning." David looks over at Franyeli, already starting to laugh.

"Say it Franyeli!" David demands of his younger sister.

"*¡Ya va!*" Franyeli laughs, playing along.

"Say it!" Daniel adds, wanting to join in the fun.

"I-an-cra-zi!" Franyeli manages to get out one syllable at a time through fits of laughter.

"Did you hear her?!" David asks Joyce, laughing harder. "She just said she is *loca*! You said you are *loca*, *Franyeli*! Say it again!"

"I know! I-an-cra-zi!" Franyeli repeats once more before surrendering herself to hysterics.

Leaving

JOYCE RAISES HERSELF up from her cot in San Juanito for the last time, at least in the foreseeable future. The little room that has been her home for the past three weeks has acquired the feel of a cozy cave. Even during the nights when she has to get up to use the restroom, Joyce can maneuver her way around the ironing board, cabinet, and random piles of clothes spilling over the different surfaces around the room. Earplugs blocked the scurrying of critters from her consciousness, and she slept better with each passing day.

The house is quiet except for the TV chatter emanating from Sara and Adan's room. The kids have already gone off to school. Joyce changes out of her pajamas and starts throwing her belongings into her backpack.

When she has finished packing, she goes across the living room and into Sara and Adan's bedroom.

Sara is still in her pajamas. She got up early to make breakfast for her husband and kids, and then went back to bed to watch TV. She will change in a few hours before she makes her way to her job cleaning a couple of apartment complexes at the bottom of the hill. Joyce joins Sara on her bed and leans back against the headboard.

"What are you watching?" Joyce asks.

"Family Court," Sara answers.

"What's the case about?"

"Argument over property. The plaintiff's sister's ex-*novio* won't move out of the plaintiff's house," Sara explains.

"Oh," Joyce settles in beside Sara, pulling the cover over her to keep out the morning chill. She and Sara watch as the host eggs on the shouting match between the plaintiff and the defendant. The host only intervenes when the two parties leave their respective podiums.

Not that different from Jerry Springer back home, Joyce thinks.

The plaintiff who owns the property starts berating her sister. "You no good *puta*. Why can't you find a decent man to take care of you and your kids?"

"You should be the one talking! Look at the lazy husband you have sponging off of you!"

"At least I'm married, instead of sinning in the eyes of God!"

When the commercials start to play, Joyce turns to Sara and asks, "Sara, why do you like these shows?" She does not understand why Sara would be interested in watching chaos when her life is already so complicated by all the family drama she is pulled into daily in San Juanito.

"It helps me think about how to deal with the situations here," Sara says. "And you realize you are not the only one with problems."

Joyce nods, tucking away the answer to process later. "So, I am leaving now," she says.

"Did you have any breakfast?"

"No, I was planning on grabbing something down at the Redoma before meeting up with the team for Tuesday prayer."

"Let me warm up a couple of *arepas* for you," Sara moves to get up from the bed.

"You don't need to do that. Really," Joyce lays her hand on Sara's arm. "You know I don't eat much in the mornings."

Sara settles back down. "Okay. If you say so. You *have* gotten a bit chubby in the last few weeks," Sara winks at Joyce.

The cursory politeness shown at the beginning of Joyce's stay has long worn off. Joyce's weight has become a standing joke between the two of them. Joyce is nowhere near overweight enough to warrant a diet, but she finds that allowing Sara to pick on her gives them something to bond over, just like with her neighbor Yasmin. It also gives her an excuse to not eat everything Sara and Adan generously offer her. If she did, she would truly be overweight.

"No, really, I'm not very hungry right now. When are you going down? Maybe we could walk together."

"I have to meet Sra. Yanet down at Blocke 13 at noon." Sara glances at the clock hanging from the wall. Joyce follows Sara's glance. Noon is still three hours away and she is ready to get back to her own apartment, her own space.

"Well, I guess I can make it down myself," Joyce says.

Going up and down San Juanito alone is no longer an issue. Ever since they came back from the beach and met every single neighbor on the way up, she has felt safe on her own, knowing that all the neighbors are *pendiente* of the *chinita*, keeping vigilant watch over her. There have been moments Joyce has wished Sara and Adan were more concerned about her safety, considering San Juanito's notoriety for crime. But she figures that if she really were in danger, neither Sara nor Adan would allow her to go out alone without an escort, even if it was just little Daniel.

The malandros are probably still asleep anyway, she comforts herself.

"Well, I'm off," Joyce says when the show ends.

"Have you packed everything already?" Sara turns her full attention to Joyce.

"*Sí.* I packed right when I got up," Joyce pauses and looks at her *tía.* The weeks have flown by. She has become one of the family, including doing her share of cooking and laundry folding. Sara has included Joyce in her life without a second thought. And now, Joyce will try to seamlessly detach herself from this family that has adopted her as a daughter, sister, friend. "I'll be back next weekend. Maybe spend the night."

"Ok, it might be a little crowded because my family from Los Telares will be visiting. But it will be fun. They'd be happy to see you again. You can stay with me in our room. My brothers will probably stay in your room."

My room, Joyce repeats to herself. She is no longer merely a guest. She is satisfied.

To Sara, she says, "I'll call you and let you know when I'll be coming up."

"Bueno."

"Thanks for everything," Joyce says, trying to sound casual.

"*A la orden*," Sara answers before turning her attention to the next episode of Family Court.

Joyce slips out of the room. As any member of a Venezuelan family would do, she does not make a big deal of her departure. Goodbyes are avoided. This much she has learned. She unlocks the front door, steps out into the *callejon*, and closes the door behind her.

She makes her way down the steps, greeting the neighbors who watch her descend safely down the hill.

Gabriel

GABRIEL WALKS SLOWLY up the hill. He does not have the Bs. 600 for the jeep ride. *Just as well,* he thinks.

His left leg bothers him. The flesh around the steel pegs holding together the pieces of broken bones has been smarting. It is infected.

A slow climb isn't as bad as having to cram into a crowded jeep with a bunch of grumpy, tired people who've had to wait for the jeeps in the rain, Gabriel thinks to himself. These people will inch however few centimeters they can away from the stench of my clothes, my wounds. People will stare at me while avoiding any human eye contact.

Gabriel is hungry. His stomach growls. He hasn't eaten for a couple of days. It is already past midnight. His mom will not be expecting him. He does not expect her to expect him. *Why will she want to? I only go home when I need something. But then, she always seems to have something waiting for me no matter how sporadically I pull my tired ass up the hill... It will make living this day worthwhile if there is a hot arepa waiting for me.*

He has had a long day.

The occasional jeep or motorcycle flies up the hill, carrying the last of the day's passengers, barely missing him. He turns into a *callejon* and starts climbing the steps one at a time. He first takes a step up with his right leg. He then drags up his left leg. *One step at a time,* he says to himself. *One step at a time.*

A light sprinkle begins to fall, sizzling on the lightbulbs that illuminate the grime running down the gutters on either side of the steps, carrying the discarded empty chip bags and plastic bottles. He is soaking wet.

He has had a long day.

Earlier, he had tried to find Julio, who owed him money for a job. Jobs are hard to come by for Gabriel. Ever since he was shot, he just can't move as fast. He is a liability. He is only good for the petty jobs.

But Julio was not home. His sister had said he had skipped out of town. She also told him that one of the leaders of the rival gang had gotten out of prison—the one Gabriel had went after a few years ago, the one he had left a bullet in. "You'd better watch your back," Julio's sister had warned before closing the door.

Gabriel had left without mentioning the money. He does not want to drag women into men's business. He has no faith in ever seeing the money.

The *callejon* is empty except for the mangy dogs. Males fight over an old bitch with tits sweeping the ground. *Damn dogs!* Gabriel curses under his breath, *Even they have someone to pass the time with.* He cannot remember the last time he felt the warmth of a woman's body. He hopes the dogs will have moved on by the time he gets to where the dogs are.

He has had a long day.

#

In the darkest hour of the night, Gabriel lies huddled in the gutter under the fading morning stars, with his bad leg sprawled across the *callejon* steps. The hunger pangs still throb through him, even more acutely than the stab wounds. He grasps at his side. Thick dark blood still oozes through his fingers, mixing with the grime and trash running down the gutter. The dogs are long gone, scared off by the running footsteps and screams. He knows they will be back. They have only retreated to some dark corner to wait for his strength to leave him completely. They will be back to gnaw at his bones. He chuckles at the image, stopping only when the pain at his side becomes unbearable. He is tired and hungry. His mom is not expecting him. He wishes she were, if only just a little.

He has had a long day.

#

The first hint of morning peeks over the horizon, uncovering the ugly secrets of the dark. News of Gabriel's murder spreads from breakfast table to breakfast table like a raging forest fire. News like this cannot be contained.

"It was coming to him."

"He deserved what he got."

"How long did he think his luck would hold out?"

"Show no pity: life for life, eye for eye, tooth for tooth."

"That's one less *malandro* in the streets."

Blame is cast, the violence held at an arm's length.

#

Lining the banks of the road, accusations join the small procession behind the corpse down the hill to stoke the fire in the furnace.

"What about forgiveness?" a child asks from behind his father's cloak.

"Forgiveness is for those who are more deserving," comes the reply.

"What about mercy and compassion?" asks a mother.

"Had he shown anyone mercy or compassion?" shouts the mob.

\#

Two other men, both criminals, were also led out with him to be executed. When they came to the place called the Skull, there they crucified him, along with the criminals—one on his right, the other on his left.

One of the criminals who hung there hurled insults at him: "Aren't you the Christ? Save yourself and us!"

But the other criminal rebuked him. "Don't you fear God, since you are under the same sentence? We are punished justly, for we are getting what our deeds deserve. But this man has done nothing wrong."

Then he said, "Jesus, remember me when you come into your kingdom."

Jesus answered him, "I tell you the truth: today you will be with me in paradise."

\#

The last nail is hammered into the coffin. Gabriel lies in its darkness, wrapped in tattered sheets stripped from his mother's bed. He has at last outrun the demons that nipped at his heels unrelentingly. Finally, he is at peace.

Judgment

EVANGELIN'S MOTHER, SRA. Beta, is surrounded by the half dozen grandchildren she parents. She has come over to Evangelin's to swap gossip.

"*¡Ay, Evangelin!* Have you heard about Gabriel? That boy who died last night?" her eyes dance behind her newly acquired, government-subsidized lenses.

"*Sí.* Enrique told me this morning," Evangelin, having just led a Bible study on not gossiping, tries her best to sound uninterested.

"That boy! You know what they say, that he had robbed his own mother. And there he was, crawling back to her. I wonder what he did this time?" Sra. Beta pauses, hoping Evangelin might fill in details she missed.

Evangelin stays silent.

"He probably got in trouble with those *malandos* down at the Redoma and was trying to stay low for a while," Sra. Beta continues speculating. "It was a good thing he didn't make it to his mother's. Just imagine him bringing more trouble to his mother's house! *¡Ay! Qué lastima!* These young men, growing up to be nothing but trouble."

"But mom," Evangelin finally speaks. "Gabriel and all those young men, what other choice do they have? You know as well as I do that his dad was a no-good cheat and his mom was so busy having babies, she had no time to raise her kids up right. Gabriel was left to fend for himself."

"Why do you go about defending those criminals? Right's right. Wrong's wrong. No matter how much his parents failed him, he still had a choice. And he chose to do wrong," With that, Sra. Beta ends the conversation.

#

The weight around Christ's ankles pulls him farther down into the burning depths of hell.

Violence

Unnamed fears
Perch on rooftops
Leak down
Stain brown streaks on dank moldy walls
Chill souls huddled within
What now?

Relentless violence
Pounds down on uneven, cracked pavements
Blasts through paper-thin, half-hearted resistance
Drills into precariously delicate sanity
What now?

What now of promises for protection?
Of miracles of deliverance?
Are they only redeemed in the next life,
After the spilt blood and the pain?

What now of unwavering hope?
Of fountains of joy?
Are they only mirages,
Locked away in the land of dreams?
What now? I ask you.

What now when children cry in their sleep from hunger?
What now when men wander the streets without work?
What now when packs of dogs roam the streets digging through trash,
scrounging for food?

What now when the rain floods away the foundation, bleeding of red earth?
What now?

Robbery

"AMELIA, CAN YOU take my bag down to the apartment?" Joyce asks across the office. "I want to go down to the Redoma to pick up some groceries."

The *barrios* are *caliente*. The increase of crime—robberies, shootings—is on everyone's minds from dawn until late into the night. Joyce does not want to risk being robbed coming up from the Redoma.

"Sure," Amelia says.

A while later, Amelia slings Joyce's bag over her shoulder. She locks up the office and starts making her way down from Las Colinas to Calle Diecinueve, thinking about the late lunch she plans to make for herself.

The day is beautiful, a perfect afternoon.

#

Amelia sees Joyce with her hands loaded with groceries at the bottom of the steps. She unlocks their apartment door. Amelia waits for Joyce to put down the grocery bags before choking out Joyce's name.

Joyce turns around and sees the distraught expression on Amelia's face. She leaves the bags of groceries on the table and wraps her arms around her friend. "What happened?"

"I was robbed," Amelia forces out the words.

"Are you okay? Were they armed?"

"No. No, they weren't armed. I don't know if they were armed. I didn't see a gun or knife. No, I'm not okay."

"What happened?" Joyce coaxes gently.

"I was walking down from the office and was turning that first corner, past the trash bin, when two guys ran out from behind those abandoned trucks. They surrounded me, one from behind, the other in front. One of them demanded that I give them your bag," Amelia's words stream out, calming her.

"I said no. Then one of them spotted my ring and tried to grab it," Amelia holds out her left hand. A delicate gold chastity ring digs into Amelia's swollen ring finger.

Joyce reaches out for Amelia's hand.

"And while one guy was grabbing the ring, the other grabbed your bag." Amelia pauses.

Joyce looks around the apartment and does not see her bag.

"And?"

"I clutched my hand tight so he couldn't get my ring, and with the other, I tried to hold onto your bag," Amelia pauses again and the blue of her eyes wells over.

"And?"

"They took your bag," Amelia says to Joyce.

"Anything else?"

"No, they took off after they grabbed your bag."

Joyce tries to process Amelia's words and finds herself emotionless to the fact that her bag was stolen. It is as if she misplaced a notebook.

"Are you sure you are alright?" Joyce asks again.

"Shaken."

"Did you see who they were?"

"No, they had pulled their shirts up to cover their faces."

"Was there anyone around?"

"There were a few kids around, just standing there, watching."

"Have you talked with Thomas or Agnes?"

"No, I ran straight here."

"We should probably let them know."

Joyce picks up their phone and hands it to Amelia. "You should call them."

She watches Amelia dial the Reeds' number and waits by Amelia's side until someone answers on the other end.

#

As Joyce unpacks the bags of groceries, her mind inventories the contents of her bag. *My notebook, address book, cell phone. Anything else? Was my camera in the bag?*

She hurries into her room and pulls open the top drawer of her dresser and moves her clothes around the spot where she usually hides the camera.

It is not there.

Crap! Why did I leave my camera in the bag? she reprimands herself. She feels a welling of undefined anxiety and anger forming in the pit of her stomach. She pushes them back down.

Breathe, her rationale instructs. *Things like this happen all the time.*

It was about time it happened to you. They are just things, her practicality counsels.

Think. Is there anything you can do? Figure out what you can do to minimize your loss, her pragmatism advises.

A reward! Her idealism pipes in.

"Let's go ask the kids whether they saw the guys and recognized who they were. Let's go tell them of a reward. Maybe I can get my stuff back," Joyce suggests to Amelia, who is lying on her bed.

"I don't want to go back up," Amelia replies, not getting up.

A part of Joyce is frustrated. She wants Amelia to help her; she wants Amelia to fight. *We have to fight the injustice, this violation. We can't just lie down and have them walk all over us!* Joyce thinks. *We have to fight back!*

But Joyce does not argue. She senses how shaken Amelia is and gives her space to rest.

Joyce goes out of the apartment and makes her way up the path Amelia had descended minutes before. She stops at the first bend in the road, next to the invasion, by the trash bin. She asks the kids playing in the playground whether they saw the robbery.

"Yes, we saw it," they say.

"Do you know who they were?"

"No, we do not."

"Well, there's a reward for returning the bag," Joyce offers, believing the kids will spread the news around the *barrios* faster than any adult could. The kids nod before returning to their games.

Joyce traces Amelia's footsteps back up to the office, passes the overflowing trash bin, passes the graveyard of trucks lining the no man's land, passes the *ranchitos* where the young men sitting outside stare blankly in front of them. The path is deserted. It is that time of the day when everyone hides from the harsh afternoon sun.

She does not feel any fear as she makes her way up the hill. Instead, her mind is preoccupied, playing out scenarios of the robbery. She imagines what she would have done—how she would have screamed and run, how she would have confronted the thieves with the love of Christ and humbled them, turning their lives around then and there.

Would I have been able to hold onto my bag had they tried to grab it from me? she wonders. *Perhaps. Perhaps they wouldn't have even bothered since they probably assumed I know karate since I am Chinese and related to Jackie Chan and Jet Li and can whoop their asses all the way to China and back!*

She entertains the whys and what-ifs. *Why did I give my bag to Amelia to carry down? If only I had taken my bag with me to the market. Why didn't I wait for Amelia to walk down together? The malandros probably wouldn't have robbed Amelia if we were together. Why didn't I take out my camera the night before like I always do? Why didn't Amelia hold on tighter to my bag?*

Only when her mind is exhausted of scenarios, only when her mind is finally quieted, does she feel. The first feeling to rise up is that of blame. Blame at the kids for not telling her who the *malandros* were—*because they know, of course they know.* Blame at Amelia for choosing to protect her ring over the bag— *because she had a choice, of course she had a choice.*

Counselor

JOYCE SITS ON her balcony and looks over the *barrios* below her. She listens to the jeeps make their way up and down the hill. She watches the children play in the streets.

Agnes walks up behind her.

"Hey, *chica*," Agnes says.

"Hey."

"Do you want to talk about it?"

"About what?"

"The robbery. You haven't said much, but you seem rattled."

Joyce looks over at Agnes and sees the gentle concern in her eyes.

"It was Amelia who was robbed, but I feel violated too," Joyce says. "And I feel guilty..."

"For what?"

"For feeling violated. It's just stuff. I'm also upset that I've been robbed of a full robbery experience so I can justifiably feel violated. I feel so defenseless. I couldn't even defend myself, my stuff, because I wasn't even there."

"Are you angry with Amelia for not protecting your bag?"

Joyce turns the question around in her mind. *Am I angry with Amelia?*

"No. I'm not angry with her, not anymore. She tried to resist. That was brave of her. There were two of them and one of her. She didn't have a chance. It's probably easier to hold your fist closed than to hold onto the strap of a bag. She is lucky she held onto her ring."

"Are you angry at God?"

"No," Joyce says automatically.

But after a minute, Joyce revises her answer, knowing her first answer did not satisfy her soul. "I don't know," she says out loud. "I mean, why can't God let me take care of my own stuff?"

She hears the anger in her own words for the first time and is struck with fear—the fear of God's wrath for doubting his will, the fear of losing her understanding of who God is, the fear of losing her faith.

But once acknowledged, she is no longer able to suppress the anger. "He doesn't even let me take care of my own stuff. He doesn't even let me take care of my own stuff!" Joyce repeats. Her anger spills over and hot tears blur her view of the *barrios*.

Agnes waits and holds each tear, each gasp for breath, each outcry in her heart until Joyce's sobs and rage finally subside.

"Joyce, nothing happens without a purpose. I don't know why this happened to you. But your feelings of injustice and violation are real. Perhaps the question isn't why God doesn't let you take care of your own stuff but why you are not asking Him to take care of *you*. Perhaps it's a good time to have a conversation with God. What do you think?"

"Crap! Excuse my profanities, but that's some serious shit you are asking me to wade into. Soul searching, faith rocking shit," Joyce says.

"What did you think being a missionary is about?" Agnes says.

"Saving souls from eternal damnation," Joyce replies with a smirk.

"Just kidding, Agnes. But you are suggesting that I never had the faith in God to take care of me, much less my stuff. And that is a serious accusation. If that is true, then I'm screwed. What am I doing here as a missionary?"

"The time you have here in Venezuela is as much about you as it is about the people you have come to care about. What happened to you may seem trivial compared to the poverty and violence you see in the *barrios*, but it is not any less relevant."

Joyce sighs and says, "There's no way around it, is there? Apparently, the faith I had in God that brought me here isn't strong enough to sustain me. I need to figure out who this God is that I believe in."

"I'm afraid though," she adds.

"What are you afraid of?" Agnes asks.

"What if..." Joyce ventures. "What if I find out that God doesn't give two shits about me? What if what I discover is worse than the reality I believe in now?"

"Do you have a choice?"

"I guess not. But I'm still afraid," Joyce says.

"I can't guarantee that your worst fears will not come true, but that has not been my personal experience when I have struggled with my faith. So when you can't believe, I will believe for you. When you no longer have hope, I will hope for you," Agnes replies.

Somehow, Agnes's words strengthen Joyce. She knows that if she ever despairs, Agnes will be there to nudge her toward the truth.

And so with Agnes watching, Joyce, in fear and trembling, takes a leap away from the faith so familiar to her and descends down the labyrinth of the unknown.

#

Around Evangelin's table, Amelia and Joyce recount their shared robbery experience. They are expecting Evangelin to show sympathy. Instead, they open a floodgate to the violations Evangelin's family has experienced, putting the robbery in perspective of the daily reality in the *barrios*.

"I was robbed at gun point Saturday morning," Evangelin says in reply.

"This past Saturday?" the girls ask, surprised that Evangelin has not mentioned it earlier.

"Yes, just a couple of days ago. I had left the house early to get to class on time in Los Telares, and a *malandro* walked up to me, held out a gun, and robbed me," Evangelin says nonchalantly.

"At least the guys who robbed me didn't have guns," Amelia says.

"Enrique was robbed last week when he was out working. He had gone up a *barrio* he wasn't familiar with. And on the way down, some *malandros* robbed him, at gun point as well," Evangelin says.

"I'm surprised neither of you had been robbed before this. Eva was robbed the first month she was here. And there was the time she came home late and got caught in the crossfire of a gang shoot-out. Fortunately, she wasn't hurt. *¡Gracias a Dios!*"

#

"My cousin was beaten up in the street. He was running away from a couple of *malandros* that were trying to rob him."

"My husband was walking home the other day and was robbed."

"My sister was killed by a stray bullet last year."

"My child was killed."

"Robbed."

"Killed."

"Injured."

"Disappeared."

Echoes of violence ricochet off the cinder blocks and through plywood walls, embedding into the hearts of the inhabitants and passersby.

Too deep to extract, they fester, oozing puss, saturating layers of balm wrapped around wounds that never heal.

#

As Joyce wrestles with her understanding and faith in God, she knows that on some subconscious level, she is not alone in her struggle. She is also taking the witness stand on behalf of the people with whom she has come to share the goodness and hope of God. She is taking the witness stand on behalf of her neighbors, on behalf of the *barrios*, on behalf of the people living in abject poverty with so little hope and so much pain and suffering.

Why, God?

Where are you?

Do you care at all?

Are we truly precious in your eyes?

As you hung on the cross, did you really die for us?

The Team

THE VIOLENCE TEARS down that invisible, invincible shield the team had imagined around them. After Amelia was robbed, Joyce was robbed again. This time, Joyce was walking down from Las Colinas to Calle Diecinueve after Tuesday morning prayer, the same path Amelia had taken when she was robbed. Agnes had accompanied her, hoping for safety in numbers. But the *barrios* are *caliente*.

None of the scenarios Joyce had played out in her head came true. She did not run off. She did not speak about the love of Christ. She did not karate-chop the *malandro*. Instead, she stood face-to-face with a young man.

The *malandro* said, "Give me your bag."

Joyce responded, "No, it's my bag."

That went on for several long seconds until the *malandro* ripped the bag from her hands and ran off.

Nothing was in the bag, just a blank notebook for notes and a pen. She had not even had the chance to make a new copy of her passport, and she had no money in the bag.

Her robbery experience was now complete.

"The streets are *caliente*," the neighbors say over and over. Waves of violence ripple through the *callejones*, sparing no one.

#

It is Tuesday morning once again. Joyce and Amelia have ascended together the road on which they both have been robbed, braving their fears and suppressing their anger. The team sits around the prayer table, silent. After a whole year without experiencing much violence in a *barrio* notorious for its

147

poverty and crime, the team had thought they had gained the respect of the *malandros* and protection of the community.

Are they not friends with Precious, the mother of all malandros who kept watch at the crossroads below the office windows? They ask themselves. Do they not exchange greetings with the young men who sit in front of their ranchitos under the sweltering heat each time they pass?

"How are you girls holding up?" Thomas asks.

Joyce and Amelia both look up, not knowing how to answer.

"It's been a tough couple of weeks, hasn't it?" Thomas says.

Joyce and Amelia nod. Agnes reaches out for the girls' hands across the table and holds them gently, praying for them in silence. She has come to love them so much and to see them hurt pierces her heart.

The touch is too much for Joyce. The brave front she is trying to present crumbles underneath the compassion. The tears start falling Joyce's eyes.

"Do you girls want to talk about it?" Thomas asks.

Joyce looks over at Amelia, who is looking down at the table not wanting to speak. So she does.

"I'm not mad at the *malandros*. At least I've been finally initiated into the *barrio*!" Joyce makes a weak attempt at humor through her tears. She likes this joke.

Since her talk with Agnes, she has wrestled with God. She has pulled her punches and aimed them at his solar plexus and has made some headway toward cooling the embers of her rage.

Amelia reaches her arm around Joyce, her companion through so much, and tries to comfort her friend.

Joyce sits under the warmth of her team's love and slowly opens up. "I'm not mad at the *malandros*. It's almost a relief in a way. I've been expecting something like this to happen, and I'm relieved that it finally has because I no longer have to wait." Joyce pauses for a second to collect her thoughts and to gather enough guts to admit the dark ugly truth of what she is about to say.

"I'm mad at God for not letting me take care of myself," Joyce takes a breath before continuing. "When I came here, I had the faith that God loves this *barrio*, loves the families we work with here. I had the faith that God watches over them. But I never had the faith that God will take care of me."

The room retreats into silence. Each person is reminded of the helplessness they have felt at one time or another since they first started on the crazy journey after Christ, to be "God's presence" in the midst of a broken and fallen world.

"Had we known what it was truly like to be crushed, to be jars of clay cracked into a million pieces so that the light of God can show through us, would any of us have followed God into the *barrios*?" they ask themselves.

"Why do the lessons of God always have to be so painful?" Joyce finally voices to no one in particular.

#

Christ, hanging from his cross, takes the accusations Joyce hurls at Him. He knows she does not know what she is doing, this beautiful child of God. He sees Joyce picking at the scabs covering her heart—the large jagged edged ones covering loss and grief, the small ones covering slights and unkind words, and the fresh one, barely starting to form over the cut left by the robberies. The wounds under the scabs fester, unable to heal. Her cries just barely revealing the pain she feels.

He takes her punches patiently, allowing Joyce to lash out in anger and pain until she grows too weak to continue.

When Joyce wears herself out, Christ looks up to God and says in a gentle voice, "It is done" and surrenders Himself to God, who casts him into the dungeon of hell to atone for the hurt and injustice the world has inflicted on Joyce.

Joyce sits at the bottom of the cross and hears Christ take his last breath. She sees with her own eyes her wounds slashed across Christ's flesh. She finally understands. With feet burning as if on hot coals, she runs to the tomb and waits for the promise of Christ's resurrection to be fulfilled, for God to finally free her from the sins of the world.

In the beginning was the Word, and the Word was with God, and the Word was God. He was with God in the beginning. Through him all things were made. Without him nothing was made that has been made. In him was life, and that life was the light of men. The light shines in the darkness, but the darkness has not understood it. (John 1)

A Conversation

GOD LOOKS ACROSS the expanse of hills blazing the gold, orange and red of the ever-expanding *barrios*. The smoke rises up out of the crevices, dank and putrid, as the fires consume the accumulated heaps of trash. Babies, soiled, cry hungrily in the corners of dirt floor *ranchitos*, for food, for attention. Young men lounge listlessly on girlfriends' couches waiting for the night. Parents, with heads bent over the kitchen table, worry about the next meal, about their sons and daughters caught in the crossfires of *malandros*, of becoming *malandros*. Old men limp up the hill on their canes, chased by jesting children. Around a small coffee table, a candle flickers. Four missionaries sit in a circle, hunched over, souls exhausted, overwhelmed by the heavy burden crashing down on their shoulders.

Before God, his angels gather. Satan is among them. But he stands apart at the edge of Heaven.

God asks Satan, His words booming across Heaven, "Why have you come? Have you come to bow before me and repent of your betrayal?"

Satan stands tall. His presence even in the bright light of Heaven cannot be dismissed as inconsequential. In his grandeur, the handiwork of God can still be seen.

Pushing his shoulders back and his chest forward, he replies, "Anything but that! I have come to show you that my powers are gaining strength. In every corner of Earth, I have penetrated deep into the souls of men. The blackness of their hearts has blocked the light of the sun. Soon, you will acknowledge the folly of your creation, and you will bow down to me."

God looks long and hard at the creature strutting proudly and arrogantly before Him. After a long pause, longer than eternity, God smiles. He replies, "Look harder."

And in that infinite passage of a second, God passes his hand over the hills, brushing away the suffocating smoke. Under the cold ashes of yesterday's blaze, the amber of hope glows, waiting to be rekindled.

Mothers coo to their babies, held gently in their arms, their breasts overflowing with honey-rich milk. Their thoughts crowd hope and a better future. Children play on the hillside, building castles out of mud and stick, dreaming of the day when they will be able to be masters of their own lives. Young men walk, erect, proud with heads held high, down the hills sprayed with wildflowers pushing up out of piles of trash. Their hearts are full of ambition and hope that today will be different from all other days; today is a new day. Families sit around dining room tables, picking out the tastiest morsels and offering them to each other. Communities gather, singing and dancing under moonlit skies, celebrating life with laughter and lightness of spirit.

Satan jeers. "All meaningless. What do these little acts show? Hope cannot withstand the drudgery of the stark reality they have to live through day in and day out."

He points his long index finger at the corners of neighborhoods where incense burns before altars to the tributes paid to gods and saints for protection. He points to the charms and amulets that decorate wrists and doorways. "These people, they have given up hope in a distant mysterious god who does not provide for them their basic necessities of safety, shelter and food. They have turned to other gods. And these gods answer their requests!" Satan says.

God stands. The magnificence of his robe fills the temple with glory. His face shines with warm light. All the angels bow before him, singing His praises with their very being. He opens his mouth and the sweet scent of jasmine fills the air.

"These are my people, my beloved. I knit each person's form in his mother's womb. I am a God ready to forgive, gracious and merciful, slow to anger and abounding in steadfast love, and I will never forsake them."

God pauses. Beams of light radiate in all directions. "I am the great I AM. In my hands, I hold all of eternity. The evil you claim to be yours, it is only but a poor reflection of what is true. The full beauty of the kingdom to come—the unveiling of which has already begun—will so overwhelm you, you will not be able to withstand its brightness."

After He speaks, God leans over and blows his spirit over the *barrios*, and the *barrios* begin to burn with a blue flame. The purifying heat scorches the hills, leaving behind beauty and joy that can only be witnessed, beauty and joy that far surpass anything ever conceived possible in the minds of men and angels alike.

"This is a faint glimpse of what you cannot comprehend!" God bellows at Satan. "Go back down and reign over your dominion. Do not boast, for your time is drawing to a close."

Satan, seething with anger, retreats into the darkness of hell with hate and resentment flaming in his eyes. God sits back down on his throne. At his right hand, a lamb lies gently in the folds of his robe. Before him, the angels worship the

God of the universe, the Alpha and the Omega, the First and the Last, the Beginning and the End.

Retreat

JOYCE AND AMELIA climb into a taxi outside the bus terminal in Valencia. Once in the taxi, the girls relax, knowing they are on the last leg of their journey. They are going on a prayer retreat at the Abadia Benedictina de San Juan for three days and two nights.

They are dropped off at the gates of the abbey by a taxi and are greeted by the security guard. They walk through the gates and onto the peaceful grounds. They check in with the *hermano* in the lobby before going to separate private rooms. They do not need to be anywhere until all the guests of the abbey meet in the dining hall for dinner.

Peace and quiet.

For the next couple of hours, both girls stay in their rooms, putting away their clothes on the clean dry shelves and the books they have lugged six hours from Caracas on the desk. They sit outside on their private balconies in solitude, looking over the green vegetation covering the expanse of the abbey grounds. They take out their journals and write down all the stray thoughts floating around in their minds. They still themselves.

When the bells ring, calling the guests to dinner, Joyce and Amelia leave their rooms refreshed and fully present. They sit amidst the guests, exchanging pleasantries until an *hermano* pushes in their dinner on a cart.

A plate of *arepas*, another plate of ham and cheese. The simplicity of the dinner cleanses Joyce and Amelia's palates.

The guests eat meditatively, chewing slowly, savoring each bite. Like Joyce and Amelia, most of the guests around the table are repeat guests and are familiar with the portions the abbey offers—just enough so you are left a tiny bit hungry, wanting just a little more. This, Joyce and Amelia both appreciate, to not be stuffed and overcome with lethargy for hours afterward.

Over the next few days, the girls mainly keep to themselves. Joyce and Amelia stick to a ritual of getting up early in order to catch breakfast, returning to bed, and waking up a couple of hours later to start their days. At least a few pages of most of the books they brought are read. Long walks are taken around the lake and through the gardens of orchids that the monks keep so perfectly. Long chats are held under the terrace where they reflect on their time together as teammates, friends and housemates, all that they have learned from each other, all that they will miss and not miss about each other. And all through those hours of personal meditation and communal reflection, the girls pray, consciously and unconsciously, listening for the voice of God to speak into those parts of them that are drained of strength and to answer the questions that keep them awake at night.

At the end of the night, before the lights are turned off and the abbey sleeps, the girls join the guests and the monks in the chapel for evening prayer. They love the evening prayer, and they savor each word of the liturgy as they do everything else at the abbey, slowly and consciously.

On the last night, Joyce finally finds the peace she does not know she is looking for.

She has already decided that she is leaving Little Steps and the *barrios*. Joyce does not doubt the goodness the ministry brings to the *barrios*. She sees the grace of God slowly unfolding in the lives of those she has worked with. And in her teammates, she cannot fail to see how they possess a passion and steadfastness in their work.

Thomas, a visionary, confidently carries within him hope that sustains him. Agnes is the realist; she leans on the passion and compassion of Christ in the face of suffering. And Amelia, the embodiment of God's blessing; her very being radiates gentleness and compassion.

However, Joyce's own reaction to the robbery has put into stark relief the reality of her relationship with God. She does not trust God to take care of her; she never did—not completely.

Joyce sees the irony of her ministry in the barrios of Caracas. She had come to Caracas believing that she was called to share God's love. But the person God has been trying to love was her. He could only do so by first showing her how little control she had over her own life. And there was no gentler way than to rob her of her defenses. Only then would Joyce be able to acknowledge that her faith was in herself rather in than God. Only then would Joyce's hands empty enough to receive God's love.

Given these empty hands, Joyce knows her time is up in Caracas. The purpose for which God had brought her has been fulfilled. She has been stripped naked. She is a vessel ready to be filled up, not poured out.

This bittersweet reality forces her to her knees. She loves her team and the families she has worked and lived with all the more because she realizes how pivotal they have been in her own journey with God. They have ministered to her.

Perhaps one day, she will return and be able to minister out of a fullness, out of an assuredness of God's presence in her life. If she is ever to be a missionary, she would not want to minister only out of the learned knowledge she has of God. She would want to minister out of the personal experience of knowing God. It is not the *saber* of God but the *conocer* of God she wants to minister from.

For now, it is enough to know that she wants to selfishly be still before the presence of God until He heals her.

Yet, she still feels a heavy burden on her heart. *What have I done besides stir up a bit of dust?* She had wondered numerous times.

While she ponders this during evening prayer on the last night of her retreat, her lips read in the prayer book,

Ahora, Señor, según tu promisa,
Puedes dejar a tu siervo irse en paz.
Porque mis ojos han visto a tu salvador,
A quien has presentado antes todos los pueblos
Luz para alumbrar a las naciones y gloria de tu pueblo Israel.

Now Lord, according to your promise,
You can release your servant to go in peace.
Because my eyes have seen your salvation
Which you have prepared in the presence of all the nations
Light to illuminate the nations and glory to your nation of Israel.

Joyce has witnessed, in all the suffering, in all the violence, God's salvation for these *barrios* she has come to call home. She has experienced her own salvation, or at least has started to, here in these *barrios*. And in that instant, her soul rises up and joins the angels in Heaven proclaiming the glory of God. In that moment, Joyce knows she is free, that her soul is free to continue on its journey, alone once again with God.

A Farewell

JOYCE MAKES HER way up the broken steps of the *callejon* toward Sra. Rosalia's, passing one last time in front of the most dilapidated *ranchito* in Calle Diecinueve. Only a couple of kids are playing in the yard.

"*¡Hola!*" Joyce greets the kids.

They skip over to the wire fence and look up curiously. "*Hola, chinita.*"

Joyce does not correct them. She has tried.

She would say, "*Me llamo Yolí.*"

They would parrot her, "Your name is Yolí."

But a few minutes later, when she continued up the *callejon*, they would yell out, "*¡Chao, chinita!*"

Joyce has always been the one and only *chinita* in these *barrios*, and *la chinita* she will remain. She reaches into her pocket and pulls out a few pieces of *chicles* and hands them to the kids through the fence. "*¿Quieres?*" Joyce asks.

The kids, not asking any questions, reach greedily for the candy.

"Tell your parents I said hi."

"*Sí,*" The kids go back to chasing each other around the dirt courtyard, remembering only the sweetness lingering in their mouths.

With that, Joyce says goodbye to them.

"*¡Chao, chinita!*" the ringing voices of the kids follow her up the steps. And with that, the kids say goodbye to Joyce.

At the top of the stairs, Joyce raps her keys against Sra. Rosalia's metal gate for the last time. Sra. Rosalia walks up from her garden below.

"Sra. Rosalia!" Joyce shouts through the gate.

"*¡Hola, mi chinita!*" Sra. Rosalia replies.

Joyce only hears the affection in Sra. Rosalia's greeting. "*Hola, Sra. Rosalia, cómo está usted?*" she replies.

"*Bien, bien.* So much work to do. Clothes to iron, floors to mop."

Sra. Rosalia opens the gate and leans forward to kiss Joyce on the cheek.

"I didn't think I'd see you again," Sra. Rosalia chides.

"I promised I'd come by today," Joyce replies, wishing she did not always feel guilty for not visiting more, and now for leaving.

She follows Sra. Rosalia to the kitchen and silently watches as Sra. Rosalia prepares coffee, her hands unconsciously moving over the stove. Joyce waits for Sra. Rosalia to speak.

"I've made a *quesillo*, would you like a piece?" Sra. Rosalia asks.

"*Sí*, of course," Joyce eyes the rich custard covered with caramelized sugar.

Joyce helps Sra. Rosalia carry the cups of coffee and the *quesillo* to the table before sitting down. She watches Sra. Rosalia cut into the *quesillo* and place a generous serving on a plate.

"*¿Para mí?*" Joyce asks as she reached out her hand to take the plate from Sra. Rosalia.

"*¡Por supuesto, mi amor!*" Sra. Rosalia nods.

"*Gracias,*" Joyce garbles the word out through a mouthful of *quesillo*. "I'm going to miss this!" She looks up to see Sra. Rosalia trembling, trying to hold back tears.

"*Ay. Mi chinita,*" Sra. Rosalia sighs and brushes back strands of hair covering Joyce's face. Joyce swallows a few tears herself. She tries to be as cheerful as she can, tries to be the best "*chinita*" she can—a *chinita* who does not say goodbye, at least not yet.

One of Sra. Rosalia's daughters comes in to wish Joyce well.

"*¡Hola, Mamá! ¡Hola, Yoli!*" she says. Her smile radiates across the room. "So you are leaving us, huh?" she teases.

"See what Joyce gave me last week?" Sra. Rosalia picks up a framed picture of Joyce and holds it up to show her daughter. She then places it back among the framed pictures of her children and grandchildren. "I have all my family around me. They come and go, but I have all my family around me, including *mi chinita.*"

Joyce pushes back down a lump of guilt forcing its way up her throat. *How do I say goodbye to this woman who has welcomed me into her life by permitting me to just be, without agenda? This woman I lounged beside on the hot days watching telenovelas? This woman who danced with me around the living room furniture, teaching me to sway to the songs of the llanos? This woman who never overfed me, never fussed over me, never treated me like a guest, but as one of the family?*

"Your Chinese granddaughter," Joyce repeats smiling at Sra. Rosalia, trying to reassure her that the invisible string that ties her to her Venezuelan grandmother will not be broken.

A Despedida

THE FAMILIES JOYCE has gotten to know during her time in Venezuela and her teammates have come to Las Colinas from San Juanito, from Calle Diecinueve, from San Miguel. They have come to say farewell to Joyce. They have gathered on the Reeds' rooftop patio overlooking the hills and valleys the team has traversed so many times over the years.

The food is laid out, simple food Joyce has grown to love. Sara has brought a chicken salad, Evangelin has made ham and cheese sandwiches, Agnes has added a cucumber salad, Edna has brought some *chucharia* from her store inventory, and Yasmin has brought a *torta de hoyama*.

Joyce had first fallen in love with Yasmin's *torta de la hoyama* ever since she tasted it at a birthday party for Yasmin's youngest almost a year ago. The pumpkin cake is more butter and sugar than anything else. For Yasmin to not only come to her *despedida* but also make her a *torta*, Joyce is touched.

The kids play, chasing each other around their parents. The adults share stories. Evangelin and Sara catch up on all the health issues in their respective *barrios*. Enrique and Adan talk about work, how much harder it is to find and how much harder they must look.

For a moment, Joyce takes in the scene before her, taking snapshots with her mind to file away with thousands of other images of life in the *barrios*. *This is my family, my extended family,* she thinks to herself. She knows she can come back here at any time in the future and naturally slide back into this community. She knows she is a part of them, and they are a part of her. There are no goodbyes, only *hasta luego*s.

A Blessing

JOYCE STANDS BESIDE Amelia at the top of the *callejon* steps in the predawn light. She watches Ramon as he pulls up in the familiar jalopy. When the car stops and the trunk pops open, Amelia helps her lift suitcases packed with *recuerditos* of cards and letters, ass-hugging jeans and polyester T-shirts into the trunk.

Joyce and Amelia hug one last time. The tears have already been shed the previous night over *arepas* with *jamón y queso duro*. They sat on their balcony looking out over their *barrios* twinkling with life. They promised to stay in touch, to call, to email, to pray for each other, to remind each other of the reality they had lived and the dreams they had dreamt.

Now Joyce opens the passenger door and settles into her seat. For a split second, she thinks she has forgotten something before she realizes she has forgotten to buckle her seatbelt. This makes her chuckle. She has finally remembered to forget. Now she will have to learn to remember again.

Joyce looks over at Ramon, her trusty *taxista* who will, for the very last time, drive her out of Caracas. She watches Ramon whisper a quick prayer under his breath and touch the plastic rosary hanging from the rearview mirror before turning on the engine. The jalopy bounces down the uneven road, weaving around the bags of trash washed down by the river of rain the night before.

The *barrio* lights blink their gentle farewell from the green hills across the valley under the early morning navy blue sky. Joyce touches the hills through the glass with the tips of her fingers, imprinting the last image of the *barrios* in her mind. She knows that she has received far more than she has given. In the *barrios*, she was given a safe space to wrestle with God until she finally submitted to Him and acknowledged her emptiness. And into that emptiness, God has poured in the love of her neighbors, the laughter of the kids. She has been a missionary ministered to by her ministry.

And just as she has experienced God's mysterious grace and mercy in her own life, she knows that God's presence will continue permeating the hearts of those living in the houses and *ranchitos* hugging the hills.

She whispers a final prayer over the *barrios*, over the families still asleep.

Now Lord, according to your promise,

You can release your servant to go in peace.

Because my eyes have seen your salvation

Which you have prepared in the presence of all the nations

Light to illuminate the nations and glory to your nation of Israel.

With this final prayer, Joyce's heart unclenches.

Post Script

From my family to Yolí,

We give thanks to God who is so far away but so close to our hearts. You sent us a friend, a sister, a companion who accepted us without limits, without conditions, in her heart, in her life, irrespective of our pasts, our class, or features of any type. She lived among us, accepted our customs. She shared with us games, studies, gatherings, oh so many things. A tie has been formed that is no different than one between family members.

The year together with you passed by so weightlessly. It seemed like just yesterday we met you. But that is the way of the Lord; that each day we learn more about Him.

He has sent us wandering missionaries, and disciples, those who teach us His word. Now, he has called our friend and sister to journey on alone, without even a family member. But she carries away with her a beautiful memory of friendship and learning.

We will remember you always and will never forget you.

We ask you, Jesus, to empower her and to bless her wherever her next destination may be. And bless her family. May the road she travels be beautiful, for the road taken shall be the road taken in service of you, Lord.

Finally, we say to her that, she is leaving our home, our family, but we will leave our doors open.

Joyce, you stay forever pressed tightly to each one of our hearts. We will always pray for you to remember the best moments.

Adan

Glossary of Spanish Words

A la orden - At your service, a phrase commonly used in place of "De nada/you're welcome"

El abasto - Corner store

La abuela - Grandmother

Apoyar – To support, to prop up

Las arepas - Corn cakes, the typical starch for a Venezuela meal

El arroz chino - Chinese fried rice

El baron - male

Basta – Enough

Bien - Good

Bien provecho – Good advantage (direct translation). When said before a meal, it means to enjoy

Beinvenidos - Welcome

La Bomba - Gas tank

La bruja – witch

Bueno – Good. Can also be used as a transitional word. Ex. Well…

Los cafecitos – small coffee

Caliente - hot

El callejon - Alley

El camaron - Shrimp

Las camionetas - Small buses

Los campesinos - The direct translation is "Farmer." However, here it is used to refer to the typical bread resembling french bread sold at bakeries.

El cancho - Sports field

Cariño - Affection

Chamo - an expression to imply "pal"

Chao – goodbye

El ceviche – a seafood dish made from fresh raw fish marinated in citrus juices and spiced with garlic or chili peppers

Los chicles – gum

La chinita – Chinese girl

La chucharia - A small store selling snacks, usually in someone's house

Los cojones – testicles (direct translation), often used to mean courage, bravery

El Comittee de Salud - Health Committee

¿Comó Estás? – How are you?

¿Comó lo hacen? – How do you make?

Conocer – to know, to be acquainted with, to be familiar with

Conozco – I know

Los conozco – I know them

La convivencia - A gathering

El cubano – The Cuban. Refers to the doctors from Cuba that are in Venezuela under the Oil for Doctors program

El cuchino – pig

Dios te bendiga – God bless you

La despedida - A send off

En la parada - at the stop

En las tiendas chinas – in the Chinese stores

La farmacia - pharmacy

La ferreateria - hardware store

La frontera – border

Gracias – thank you

Gringo(a) – American

La guanavana – soursop

La guayaba - guava

Haga me arroz chino – make me Chinese rice

Hallacas - a version of the corn tamal stuffed with a stew of
meats and adorned with raisins, capers, olives

Hasta luego – see you later

Hecho en China – made in China

Hermanos(as) – brothers (sisters)

Hijo(a) – son (daughter)

Hola - hello

El hoyama – pumpkin

El jefe - boss

La lechosa - Papaya

Listo - Ready

El lobo – the wolf

Loca – crazy

Los llanos – the plains of Venezuela. Also refers to a kind of
music that originated in the plains

Los malandros - thugs

La masa – dough

Me llamo – my name is

Mi amor – my love

Mi chinita preciosa – my precious little Chinese girl

Mi chinita, mi bella, mi corazon – my little Chinese girl, my
beautiful, my heart. These are phrases of affection often
heard in the streets

Misioneras – missionaries (female)

Misioneros - missionaries

La mora - Raspberry Platanos – plantains

No sé – I don't know

No te preocupes – do not worry

La novia - girlfriend

El novio – boyfriend

¡Ojalá! – God willing

Oof! – an exasperation

El pan de jamón – a Christmas pastry filled with ham

La panaderia – bakery

Panas – slang for pals

Papá – father

Para mí – for me

Pendiente - Mindful of

Picante – spicy hot

Piecitos De Dios – Little Steps of God

El platano - plantain

Por supuesto - of course

Los primos –cousins

Puta – Slut (slang)

El ranchito – shack

Que chévere – Cool, nice

Que lástima - What a shame

Qué quieres? – What do you want?

El quesillo – custard made from sugar, eggs and condensed
    milk. Similar to the Mexican flan

El queso duro – hard cheese

¿Quien? - who

Quién es? – Who is it?

Los recuerditos – keepsakes

Saber – to know, to learn, to find out, to have factual
    knowledge of

Saluda a tu mamá para mí (para nosotros) – greet your mom
   for me (for us)
El sanalotodo - Medicinal herb
El santero – witch doctor
La Semana Santa - Easter week
Sí - yes
Lo siento – I'm sorry
Son los malandros – they are thugs
La taxista – taxi driver
La telenovela – soap opera
La tia - aunt
Los tios – Aunts/Uncles
La torta del hoyama - Pumpkin cake
La tranferencia - Underground transfer tunnel
Vamanos, Yolí, Vamanos a jugar – Let us go, Yolí, Let us go
   play
Ve en paz – go in peace
Viste – Did you see?
Ya - Direct translation, "already." Also used similarly to basta
¡Ya va! - Expression similar to "All right! "Hold on!" "I'm
   coming!"
Ven – Come (a command)
Yo también - Me too